D1742855

2Killer Bytes

"Who controls the past controls the future:
who controls the present controls the past"

George Orwell

A DCI Jarrod Fischer Novel

By

F.J. Hardý

NB All reasonable efforts have been made have been made
to contact the copyright holders Bicycle Music Publishing
for using a verse of the song Fortunate Son.
Title:2Killer Bytes
Author: F.J. Hardý
Publisher: Domeday Books
Address: POBox 8625, Norfolk, VA 23503 USA
ISBN: 978-1-73257-301-7

2Killer Bytes

Acknowledgemts

Special Thanks to:

My lovely daughters Annie & Lizzie, Mum,
Seika Smith, Kara Hughes for her kind help in
proofing and suggestions,
Jax x, Jo Q, Nik Orr, Paul & Matt M at work,
the Worthing Police for their hints and help,
Fr Stephen & Fr Felix for their input,
Donna Pullen, Nick Battershill, Fi & Derrick,
Mark Caplan and Llanwoeseth Mardis.

Preface

Iraq. Operation Iraqi Freedom.
Approximately 50 clicks west of Tikrit
April 2003 22.45 hours Zulu time.

The light of the Moon bathed and caressed the desert floor like an ocean as it had done for eons. The moonlight covering the soft ground cooled it ready for the heat of the next day. The sand that always seemed to cleanse itself of the armies that had come to fight over this region throughout history who had then in turn fought, bled and died only to have their bones and detritus of war buried and reclaimed by the earth as though swallowed by some devouring beast that lurked unseen beneath the sand. Tonight was another such night of battle being fought by warring armies as those soldiers before that had stretched back through the mists of time had done *like Cambyses himself who vanished with his army en route to the Oasis of Siwa and destroy the Temple of Amun but disappeared in a sandstorm.* Only the means of transport and the weapons had changed. The sound of the Blackhawks in formation carrying their warriors grew in the still night air. As the helicopters gradually descended the rotor blades whipped up clouds of sand before the soldiers left the safety of their Blackhawks. This night would not be the last night that Death's shadow crossed this ancient land and made its presence known....

1

Present Day

It was a quiet early October morning as Darren entered through the double doors to the call centre floor. The noise of the cleaners, singing along to their iPods as they cleaned the desks and vacuumed the floor. Darren received barely a glance from them. Not that he cared. He was quite happy to melt into the background. Darren had been with Carewise Appliances for six years now, rising with speed to deputy team leader on Ali's team - a company based in Brighton that sold cover for home appliances – after having worked for various IT firms. By chance one day he had had, a meeting with a friend who worked for them and told Darren that Carewise were looking for staff, and Darren had leapt at the chance. He was happy in his job where he was helping Ali with the day to day running of the team dealing with things such as logging results, call listening, team coaching, listening to problems. Both with work and occasionally of a personal nature and other help that Ali needed. He liked Ali and Ali always greeted him warmly with a smile when he arrived.

"You okay, chap?" said Ali as Darren started to get ready for his day.

"Yeah, as always Ali, ready to start the day," Darren said, with the 'let's start work' tone that Ali wished the rest of his team could adopt.

Ali was busy cleaning the team details off the wipe board, so the new team information could put up, showing the highs and lows of another busy day at Carewise. Since Ali had been team leader, his team had always ended up in the top four. Darren *ALWAYS* made sure of that.

Darren started to log on his system ready for the day ahead. Today, Darren had other things on his mind. Not his relationship with Tash, but a tip he'd got from one of his friends. *Anyone who saw Darren would have noticed he was on edge today, but when you're selling aren't you always on edge?* What a lot of people did not know that, as soon as Darren got out of work he would rush home to his computer. Not to surf, but to hack. Many people would be nervous at the thought of someone hacking into their computers, but Darren didn't care. He'd already hacked into payroll, improved his salary and, massaged the stats for the team. No wonder he could afford to go to nice places on holiday with Tash. Butlins? Thought Darren. Fuck off! Thailand for us again. He smiled as others asked how he was able to do it every year. Darren told them he'd had a huge inheritance which was there for a rainy day. *If only they fucking knew,* he said smiling to himself.

Darren sat nervously at his desk. A tense nervous knot tightened inside him, A mixture of fear & excitement. He looked around the office. The signs above the teams - 'Sam's Sharks,' 'Matt's Mashers,' 'Becca's Bunnies,' 'Tara's Angels'- were amongst those in the office. He looked round. He could see Tash at her desk. Tash had always been involved in customer service. Even though she had been a bright student with eight O levels at either an A or B she enjoyed working with the public. Her parents were

in well placed jobs and had often tried to get her well positioned jobs but as they realised if that what made Tash happy was working with the public then they let her be. Tash had been at Carewise a bit longer than Darren, but she was good at her job, getting good sales every month without any help. She would often twirl a pen in her shoulder length honey blonde hair while she was talking. However, a few years before she had been let off with a caution by the Police after a Breach of the Peace in the town after a team night out. They smiled at each other as lovers do. Tash and Darren had been going out since the day he made a cheeky pass at her in the staff room. They liked each other a lot and were well suited to each other. They would spend all their time together and then, one day, he hoped to ask her to marry him and that's why he always carried an engagement ring with him just in case.
He listened to the voices on the call floor, a never-ending sea of noise.

"Mr Ryan, I can see you haven't got cover for your TV. Yes, it's £26 per month and yes, you do get accidental damage...."

"Hello? Mr Davies? Are you still there…………? Fuck you."
"Good Morning Mr Hardy, just a quick call to say that the cover on your washing machine is coming up for renewal. Have you? Oh, ok well enjoy the rest of your day then."

"Oh, you're so lucky Mrs Peters with your insurance that you've bought today and if you need any more help just ask for Rama."

Darren's mind drifted back to the day his parents had bought him his first home computer. He was hooked. It wasn't an all singing all dancing one, but it gave him a taste for computing. Instead of watching TV or having his head in silly magazines he'd be in his room with his computer for which his parents were happy. From then on, he read every computing magazine he could get his hands on and slowly, but surely, he began to get his head round learning how to program the computer and what made a computer tick. They were simple programs but each one a little bit more difficult than the last, teaching him about how to program. After a while he got another computer, more powerful than this one, and then another one better than the last.

Darren would go to the local computer exhibitions learning what the latest chips were and speaking to the industry reps. It was at one of these exhibitions that he met Warren or The Waz as he was more commonly known. They were to become firm friends. They would often watch films about computers & hackers and, by watching a film Darren found out that not only did Warren have contempt for the way Hollywood would portray hackers, such as how they all liked obscure characters and played role playing games or started WWIII from fancy bedrooms, but Warren revealed he was a hacker himself. Darren thought, *'Oh yes'* in that *tell me another one it's got bells on way*. It wasn't until Warren showed him how he could hack into Brighton Council that he believed him. From time to time Warren would often pass him, tips on different sites of interest which Warren thought Darren would like.

The day passed slowly. Darren would peek at his watch wishing it was closer to home time.

"You okay, big fella?" Ali asked as he often played with his greying beard or sometimes fiddled with his glasses.

Like Darren, Ali had not been with Carewise a long time. Around ten years but had been previously in the RAF seeing service during the Kosovo Crisis of the late 90s and had been at the airport during a **VERY** tense standoff with the Russians. He joined soon after his discharge and had become a team leader of which he was happy to be.

"Just not feeling all that well Mate," replied Darren who, could hardly tell Ali that he was looking forward to hacking somewhere.

"Want to go home?" Ali asked.

"I'll be good, thanks, Ali," Darren said.

"Ok big guy!! But if you do let me know!" Ali said thoughtfully.

The hours passed slowly, gradually the hand crept towards going home time. Darren breathed a sigh of relief as he logged off his computer. He walked towards the door joining others in a walk to the lifts or down the stairs. He smiled towards Tash as she gave a smile back and waved, while talking to some client. He thought Tash was good at her job and didn't need to help her figures. All the way home on the bus he was nervous; listening to the band on his mobile, tapping the beat on his back pack that he was holding on his lap.

He got off the bus and walked quickly but nervously to his front door. Inside, he threw his jacket and backpack on the sofa. He'd no reason to rush tonight as he had a few days off. Perfect he thought as he got ready to have a shower, something to eat and then later he would start looking at the tip his friend Warren had given him.

It was an unwritten rule that no one asks - to quote a phrase - no questions no pack drill - no investigating where you got the tip from. He threw the paper on the desk near the keyboard as he walked to the kitchen. Darren had been in his place over a year, ever since his mum had died and left him some money, which enabled him to buy the house outright with some money still left over. He sat down and turned on his 42" wall mounted TV, watching some sports programme. He jokingly thought about how Hollywood would make a film of him someday and who would play him. Hmmm what a thought!!! Maybe Ben Affleck!

Later he turned on his computer and began to prepare his routes. If you're going to hack into a system you never go direct. Always find different ways in so, that there is no opportunity for you to be traced. Just before he typed in the entrance code he paused. Nerves? No, it was just a way to focus on what he was about to do. Each time he gained entry he was always cautious and never rushed into a new site without looking at the 'back door' first.

As the new host site opened he wasn't surprised, it was a standard company site. Nothing that was exciting here or, so it seemed. He looked at the phone numbers, especially the area codes. Use of language. Now, he was convinced he was in the real company site. He started to look for the file he was looking for. He went to one file that linked to yet another one. It was to Darren the 21st century equivalent of following a trail of breadcrumbs. In this case, cyber breadcrumbs. He found the file he was looking for buried in a standard routine file. The two words of the title stood out bold and dark like the subject itself. He gasped, froze in disbelief. So, it was real after all he thought to himself. The stories, rumours of this project had been just that. Rumours and theories. The many documentaries that have been made on the subject were true even the input from that well-known guy who had been in the MOD. The sceptics had done their part and were well paid with their thirty pieces of silver for their part in this conspiracy. Was this a government plan to spread confusion by hiding things in plain sight?

Once again, he checked the file. After a while of looking at pages with schematics, listings of people and other information Darren was now convinced this was real. Kind of like the Holy Grail of hacking. He focused on what he was doing, and he started reaching for the drawer that contained his supply of memory sticks, and before making copies he began to set up each with its log on or, as Darren called it, 'The Gate.' A gate was so that if anyone found the stick it would be impossible for them to enter without the password but this one used a page from a newspaper which few people knew about. Darren was careful with the choice of password, making copies, still shocked and numb with the enormity of the scale of what he'd just found.

2 Killer Bytes

All the stories, the speculation and rumours of this project had until now been just that rumours and theories. Later, after a few hours, he finished and logged out of the site. Turning in his chair and facing the windows as he drew on his vape, He let out the mist in a large cloud he wasn't really paying attention and still trying to take in the enormity of what he'd seen. He put his memory stick in a safe place taped behind a cabinet in the living room. 'My insurance,' he said softly but nervously.

Sitting back in his chair his mind drifted back to his girl. As he sat back his Cat Mr Ben jumped on his lap purring softly. Darren began to stroke the cat who enjoyed being on his master's lap.

"What have you been up to, my lovely fuzzball?" he gently said to the cat who was softly purring, and stroking it as he slowly started to get up from his chair to go up the stairs and to bed.

2

"In wartime, **truth is so precious** that she should always be attended by a bodyguard of lies."

Winston Churchill

In the Tribeca area of New York, there are many streets. Some are busy and, like this one, quiet and run down. The sort that barely see people and empty cans that can dance along the ground in the wind without being disturbed and the only sound are the empty cans making a hollow rattling sound as they dance in the wind. There is a shop front not unlike any others in this street with dirty stained frosted windows a light that can be seen in the window burning all the time like a welcoming beacon through the dirty opaque window.

It was something the owners liked, the dirtier the better. Also, the window had seen many posters pasted on over the years. Some tatty and torn and others, quite recent. Above the window was the hoarding advertising 'Solomon's Trading Inc. Est 1920' the stained fonts in Hebrew and Roman - along with the Star of David - both said the same message: that visitors must make an appointment beforehand, again covered by the patina of dirt, smog and dust, thanks to the years of deliberate neglect.

If someone had managed to open the door, then they would have been confronted by two burly security guards who would politely but, in a firm way, thank the enquiring visitor and suggest that there were other trading firms that were less busy and would readily welcome their business elsewhere in the city.

If they were very lucky and managed to get passed the guards they would have been impressed with the state-of-the-art biometric security door something that was more akin to something found in a nuclear missile silo. Once through they would have walked along a corridor to a single door then, once through this door they would have had to turn right as there is a security wall to prevent people from seeing what was inside the room as they opened the door. Once in the room they would have been surprised at the number of monitors showing different regions of the world. Various types of symbols denoted different assets. Military and civilian. Some monitors also showing footage from drones and CCTV.

Kyle was one such operator. He'd been a bright promising student at MIT. MIT the prestigious University in Cambridge Massachusetts. Founded in 1861 to deal with the increasing industrialization of the United States and many famous people including Buzz Aldrin and Kofi Anin had attended and were listed amongst the roll call of famous alumni. It was while he was there that he'd been talent spotted by a lecturer who had links with certain US government agencies.

Similar to the way the Spooks in Britain are recruited through MI6, although they would have welcomed the gift of hindsight regarding one Guy Francis de Moncy Burgess before he'd been spotted at Trinity College Cambridge who ended up spying for Russia during his time at Six and was one of the 'celebrity' group of defectors that ended up living in Moscow.

Seen that Kyle was the sort of candidate that would fit in he was then approached one morning after a lecture by the type of people in dark clothes and untraceable cars. Given the 'doing your bit for your country' speech he had eagerly signed the contract. In a way he saw his job as defending the country he loved as much as a grunt on the frontline and to avenge his older brother Ryan who had been killed on duty while serving in Iraq during Operation Iraqi Freedom some years before.

On his desk he had the picture of both him and his brother before he was deployed for the last time. His role was to monitor various websites of interest that belonged to the American government or had links, though tenuous, to it and to make sure they were safe from foreign intrusion. Some days were busy others, like today, were quiet that was until a little buzzer and flashing light told him there had been a hack. He started going through the check list. What had been the target? What files had been compromised? More importantly, the origin of the hack. Kyle thought nothing of what had been hacked but the effort to trace this character.

"He's good," Kyle said with a smile, "but not as good as me. Aaah, this dude's in Brighton, England!"

After fifteen minutes he'd got all the information he needed. Made his report and sent it to his line manager. That was done. Back to his job and, what happened next, was not his concern but, his job was to defend the sites his country held as vital.

His line manager sat at his desk looking at the information Kyle had got on this character. What a waste he thought as he sent the report higher up the chain.

Eventually, the report made its way to a quiet and yet out of the way office in Washington DC. The man, or, Controller as he was known, sat behind a desk, reading reports as they came in by email. He was authoritive looking to anyone who came to his office. The dark three-piece suit with white shirt. The only concession was the range of colourful ties he wore. His grey hair short, smart and never a hair out of place. He reached Kyle's report. Ten minutes later he sat back in his leather chair, turned to the window and breathed out angrily before folding his hands as if in prayer to his face and, after a few moments in contemplative thought he began to react. He paused to pick up the battered metal mug with its regimental badge of a double ended match to sip his coffee. He started to send emails out to various individuals. He paused, should he send one to Greg? For now, he paused. Thought carefully but decided not to. His emails were as simple as the taste of décor in his office which was how liked to keep things. Then, he looked up a booking form order to arrange a room for the meeting. Everyone in the group. There were twelve. Always twelve from the beginning a group to deal with the running of covert dealings within the US Government. Biblical in a way but, that's how it had been. He sent an email to attend. It wasn't a case of not wanting to but, they must.

2 Killer Bytes

The next evening the room was ready. It was a quiet room. Little care or attention had been taken over the years with the décor in the meeting room but then it wasn't for social activities. The walnut effect table stained and worn through years of use had been a long time out of fashion as were the chairs that surrounded it. The only compromise was a print, faded, but of a sailing boat from the early 1800s. The sort of print that had once been the vogue many years ago. The Controller had made copies of the information earlier and began to place them on the table, so members of the group would have the details to hand. He knew that once the meeting was over he would ensure each file was collected and destroyed as the information contained was so explosive that it would start proceedings that would make Watergate look like Sunday afternoon tea with a priest. The people started to enter, some not all that happy at having to cancel out of work events at such short notice. They sat down with refreshments that had been provided by the Controller.

"I'd like to start by saying thank you all for coming. I appreciate you giving up your time to meet me," said the Controller.

A few rumblings from the gathering came from round the table.

"A short time ago, we experienced a hack into shall we say, one of the important files of a well-known organisation," he continued.

"I've taken the liberty of printing out what was hacked and, the details of the person who did this for you to look at."

The group started to go through the files. Some sat reading no doubt thinking of raising questions over the expenditure but thought the better of it. A Senator from the Mid-West put down the file and motioned to the controller.

"Yes, Senator?"

"Do you mean to tell me that I've given up a meeting with those who elected me to come and read something my wife can pick up by the checkout when she goes shopping?" The Mid-West Senator demanded.

"Firstly, I think you mean the meeting with your secretary in a motel and secondly, this isn't something that can be found in any of the tabloids, Senator. Maybe I could suggest to your wife that she would like to help you at your future meetings?" the controller replied.

The Senator sat back, fuming, realising he'd been found out and making a mental note to replace his secretary.

"People, you've known me for a long time. You know that I never ventured into fiction. I've always only given you the facts. Despite what you've heard in certain shows on TV this IS the real deal. Yes, we have lied and deceived our people but only because it has been necessary for National Security." The controller paused to let his words sink in.

How many times had this phrase been used over the years? It was like the phrase at Nuremberg that people wanted to be excused from the guilt of sickening crimes they had carried out by saying they were only following the orders of a superior officer.

People shifted in their seats knowing what the controller had said was true. A decision had to be made. What was going to be done next? A quiet man with untidy dark hair that was starting to go grey and sitting quietly in the corner, carefully adjusting his glasses spoke next.

"I've read this. I know it's real. I've worked on the project out west and helped with disinformation especially on myself. Even though the media caught sight of my payslip with our tax code on it was quickly dismissed and now it's been largely forgotten. If this was to get out the outcry in the papers would cause problems for years to come. We cannot afford to let this get out in the public domain as you can imagine the fallout. The years we've spent debunking this for it to be confirmed would be a disaster. What would happen? For one, there would be a huge inquiry. The Senate would have their work cut out on the eternally ongoing meetings just to set up an inquiry. We've used our caretaker Greg before. Isn't he getting a little bored just watching the ocean every day?" the man said.

The group murmured in agreement with each other. The outcome of the vote was as one. The hacker had to be dealt with. Greg had a new job. As they were leaving The Controller collected the folders and put them in the flap of the incinerator. He sat down and, reaching inside his jacket pocket, found his secure mobile phone. He knew Greg wouldn't pick the message up right now but later. He typed the message as quickly as he could. He sometimes envied the young, how quickly they can text their friends with their modern phones and tablets. He could now relax just a little as the soft, near silent ping came from the phone to tell him the message had been sent. Just tidy up the office. Home and then, the luxury of sleep.

The next morning, in Florida where it's warm and sunnier than in Washington, D.C., a man sits on the porch of his seaside home. Every day, the same chair, the same bottle of tequila. To those that wandered by, if they waved at Greg, he'd always wave back, and they would envy how calm he looked. The faded shirt, the shades that seemed to sit on his black, yet, slightly greying beard the old worn straw hat every inch the 'Beach bum' image that he cultivated. Not bad for an Army veteran. For his age and average build, he'd kept himself in good shape. A good cover. Nobody would guess that in the old desk drawer near his mobile, was a special Glock that was silenced and always loaded.

He put his glass of tequila down and turned on his mobile. A bell rang to say that there was an incoming message. He opened the message, a wry smile formed on his face. Greg went inside his house to where he had his laptop. As he waited for it to warm up and start he rubbed his left upper arm to where his tattoo of a dagger was. Not just any dagger but, those favoured by certain units of the American forces that would like not to get any publicity.

Greg had been in the army a long time. Typical of so many kids without any direction. The talk by the visiting recruiting sergeant at his college had started him on the path to the army. Greg had been an only child, he had a good childhood playing with his friends, also a normal relationship with his parents but as he grew older he'd become restless growing gradually away from the church. His father had been a Vietnam vet and had often hoped his son would join the army. His father wasn't disappointed as he saw Greg at his passing out parade only a few months before passing away from lung cancer.

Greg spent an hour reading his message, thinking about it before confirming he was ready for work. Later he sat on the porch watching the sea in its endless cycle before getting ready for his trip.

3

Darren had already left a message for Warren and they agreed to meet up later the next day for a coffee in of the many cafes in Brighton's South Lanes. It was one their regular haunts as it was public, warm and cosy and when they talked, nobody could hear them over the background noise of cups being put down on saucers and the other customers talking to each other.

The sound of the radio also helped, and they always sat near the speakers of the radio tuned into one of the local radio stations which added to the atmosphere so if anyone did try to hear they couldn't hear anything that Darren and Warren were saying.

"So, what did you think? Was it the real deal?" said Warren excitedly.

"You don't know?" said Darren.

"I thought you'd like to see it first for a change dude! I had an idea what it was about but this time I thought you could take first look!" Warren said.

Hmm, thought Darren, his loss but I suppose fair is fair.

"I've made a copy. I mean, well, in case something should happen. This time it's big. Bigger than anything I've seen so far. It's amazing, literally out of this world man. All those experts on TV saying it was real and others debunking it and I thought the documentaries were just for entertainment. I mean can you imagine how famous we'd be if we went public," Darren said excitedly.

"Or very much dead? Thought about that mate? If it's what I think it is I think we might end up feeding the fishes and I for one, don't intend to be fish food! If we keep shtum and have it for ourselves and not tell anyone, we'll be okay," said Warren who was starting to tremble with apprehension, realising now that this was getting way out of both their depths.

In way too deep. Hacking into the Council system and other companies for fun was one thing and, a bit of profit was one another, but hacking into a well-known organisation especially in America, and taking something that was meant to be hidden was definitely another matter. These days you never knew, despite all the safeguards you took, whether you were being observed or not.
Darren pushed the memory stick slowly across the table towards his friend. Warren sat there nervously debating whether he should be thinking of taking it. He paused. Should he, or shouldn't he? Slowly, his hand reached forward. His hand paused in mid-air above the stick debating within himself what he should do. Seconds later his mind made up he quickly reached forward, grabbed it, and put the memory stick in his pocket. If he had known what was going to happen next, he'd have never even taken the tip to give to Darren let alone take that innocent looking device. They continued their coffee and chatted about upcoming films, girls and the next match that Brighton were going to play.

After a while Warren and Darren left the warmth and security that the café offered and wandered off to Darren's home to play computer games. While they were talking, a man, in a beachside home far away was packing his bags. He was no stranger to this. He knew the drill. If he had his bag opened at customs or as it went through the scanners he'd have no worries as all it contained were the things a tourist would have. He was careful yet, in the back of his mind he knew how careful he'd have to be as one tiny slip could blow this open and then, the shit could really hit the fan. He destroyed all the documents that had been sent and printed out and then used a special app on his laptop to delete the emails to make sure that if anyone tried to look for them then they would never have known that they had ever even existed. He knew things were secure but these days you could never tell who could be reading what and the level of sophistication especially with computers was improving by leaps and bounds on a daily basis.

Greg spent the rest of the time relaxing by tinkering with one of his favourite cars. Always cleaning and polishing the car. Making sure the engine was good. He favoured his Jaguar. It was something about a European car that stood out from any other country. The purr of the engine as it was just idling, the cut and smell of the seats and the layout. He never drove it much. Only a short distance just to make sure everything was working and ticking over as it should. He paused for a coffee sat down while he was drinking his coffee and looked at a photo on the wall of the garage of a group of men in military fatigues and guns standing next to a Humvee he smiled as he put his thumb on two of them as many a vet does when they remember fallen comrades. There was also a picture of him with his dad when he was little on a beach, the name of which had long faded in time all he remembered were the happy times he'd spent with his dad who spent his time with him and had read Greg a story when he was little before going to sleep. He'd been with the firm since the end of Operation Iraqi Freedom and had been one of their best Kites. A Kite was a person used by 'The Firm' but if anything went wrong they could always cut the strings, so they could deny all knowledge of what had happened. Much like the old Mission Impossible TV series where if the protagonists were caught they would be disavowed. But in Greg's case the Firm could never be sure.

In the next few days he was on his way. The letter with his attorney just in case. Together with a package should anything happen to him. He had been working for the firm for some time, but he thought it would be dumb not to have a little insurance.

He'd flown the Atlantic many times, so he was relaxed as the plane flew high, speeding towards England. Catching some sleep. Not long but always drifting in and out. The firm knew his work that's why they never set any time limits as like the Mounties, he always got his man.

The sound of the Pilot telling everyone that the plane was approaching Heathrow woke him up giving a brief description of the weather in London before wishing those on board a pleasant time. After a while the plane had taxied to a halt for disembarkation and the passengers had started to leave the plane in the usual noisy touristy way. Greg wasn't like the rest. Why would he have to rush? If they knew why he was here then, the other passengers might be justifiably nervous as the thought of having a hitman sitting next to them while flying across the Atlantic isn't the most reassuring thing. After breezing through immigration, he first went to get a coffee. Greg sat at one of the many cafés at Heathrow quietly drinking a hot black Americano and let the caffeine surge through his tired veins the smell and the taste of the hot coffee hitting his taste buds slowly waking him up, watching the people about their business. It was one of the things he did watching people, seeing them rush around like nervous ants worrying about mostly insignificant things like whether they had packed a certain book, or did they remember to get a present or did they cancel the milk.

After finishing his coffee Greg went to get a snack for later. One of those cartons of coffee and what the British erroneously (in his mind) called a sandwich. Boy, how he wanted to tell them what they were missing out in the States, unlike the soggy bead and 'finely sliced' fillings that the British thought a quality sandwich was despite the fancy description and how they should learn to make a proper sandwich. He went and hired a car and, an hour later he was heading to his first port of call which was a storage unit near Horsham. He always used the same storage unit as it would be where he'd pick up the items the company gave him for his job.

When he stopped at a roadside café for a comfort break, he took the time to send a text to the Controller letting him know that he had landed safely and was en route to collect the items from the storage locker. The controller read this and a part of him started to relax. He put the phone down knowing Greg would do what the 'firm' was paying him to do. He started to work on the problem of how to fix the website so there would be no more hacks. He sat in his chair his fingers forming a roof like a little chapel as though in prayer and his mind focusing on the steps needed to fix the site so that there would be no more unauthorised access.

Greg eventually arrived at the storage unit and parked in the car park. It was one of those units that had sprung up very quickly. Metal sheets folded like corrugated card painted in a colour that was friendly to the eye and the environment so that anyone passing would barely glance and would not want to stop and look at. The company name 'Sammy's Storage' with a picture of a squirrel above the entrance welcoming people. As Greg walked inside he passed the company products. Cardboard boxes of all shapes and sizes, wrapping paper, different types of bubble wrap and rolls of tape, prices of how much it would cost to hire.

 Adverts showing what a great place it was to store anything you needed. Greg breezed in. Going through the corridor listening to the muzak that was being played in the background and how he could go in any type of store in any country all over the world and hear virtually the same muzak. He wondered if people would really notice if there wasn't any? Framed pictures taken from photo stores of staged smiling actors trying to be customer service agents with their faked smiles looking relaxed and well dressed. Greg thought Are they really that relaxed? Do people really take notice of them? All fake but there just to give people a feeling that they were being looked after. Inside it was full of storage containers some big and some small. It was no problem. He knew the drill so that whatever he needed was untraceable. No question of the firm being held accountable if anything was seized. He opened the door to the locker and looked inside. There was a large envelope and various boxes. He carefully opened each one inside the large locker making sure the CCTV would not see what was inside. Inside one was a Glock 17 that had all references erased along with a silencer and five magazines, plus another box with a supply of bullets. Greg was never surprised at how much they gave him.

He jokingly thought to himself he could fight a small third world banana republic with the ammunition the firm had issued him. He looked at the witness holes in the magazines. Not that he doubted they were full but, just out of habit. Other boxes contained large sums of money. Greg knew the bean counters at the firm would still like to account for every dollar spent. Satisfied, Greg put everything in his bag and then closed the now empty locker and left the building. He then drove off to find a quiet place and stop where he could read the information in peace and no camera could record him doing so.

He later found a quiet out of the way place pulled the car over stopped the engine and opened the carton of coffee. Greg shuddered at the taste. Vile, but drinkable. He was amazed at how the Brits drank this stuff without complaining. Reading without emotion about what Darren had done. Details of where he lived and, also his job. Greg had already begun to work out a rough idea how to deal with him and see what information Darren had in his possession then make sure it was destroyed. Now, all he had to do was to get to Brighton.

Greg arrived in Brighton later that afternoon. He'd been given the address of a bed and breakfast near the seafront where he could base himself Greg then made the arrangements for the hire car to be collected as it would attract unwanted attention. He told the owner of the bed and breakfast he would need the room for some time and would pay for the month as he was over in Brighton trying to trace his ancestors and he was unsure how long it would take, going to his room with his bags he locked the door, taking the Glock he put it under his pillow and showered to rid himself of the grime of travelling and to feel fresh again. He put on his pyjamas and let himself drift into the welcoming nirvana of sleep.

Flash! Bang! The sickening smell of cordite. The staccato sound of gunfire in the night as the sand settled around him falling to his face seeing the muzzle flash to his right.

"Ryan, Get the fucker with that machine gun. Two o'clock Bro!"

The sound of knocking on the door woke Greg up he sat up, covered in sweat, he realised he'd been dreaming again.

"Is everything all okay Mr Parker?" the voice asked.

"Yeah! I'm okay, just a bad dream that's all, thanks," Greg replied.

Greg smiled to himself. The touch of irony. He had when he arrived, signed himself in under the alias of Robert Leroy Parker. The old West had always held a fascination for Greg. The heroes and villains. Stories of famous towns like Tombstone, Dodge City and Deadwood. As a kid he'd dress up as a cowboy and play for hours with his friends. The story of Butch Cassidy and The Sundance Kid and how the over romanticised legend grew of them being latter day Robin Hoods robbing from the rich to give to the poor. While in reality it was more like that they robbed everyone to give to themselves, missing out on the poor, but he guessed they were working on how to give their ill-gotten gains out to the masses. How they finally met their end in South America in a heroic last stand as the movie would depict. Then there was a theory that they didn't die but returned to the States quietly to live out their days. He thought of what Butch would say if he knew the irony of using his real name as an alias. Greg thought that Butch would find it very amusing to say the least.

He woke up later. Feeling refreshed despite the nightmare from the past. He washed and got ready for 'work'. He took the Glock and carried it with him in his jacket. After breakfast he went to town and got himself a small map of Brighton along with a bus timetable and other essentials. Greg sent a short text to confirm all was okay. He then returned to his room with his shopping. Soon he had set up, to anyone who came to clean the room, what was a small office. If anyone had asked he'd just say that he was tracing his ancestors. He knew the British liked hearing that from Americans and that they would do anything to help.

Greg later took a walk along the seafront. A far cry from the warm Florida beach and the house he lived in. He faced the wild sea with its waves crashing on the shore the sound of the sea shimmering as it drew back through the pebbles.

He stood there the wind blowing through his hair. His eyes closed savouring the smell and the rawness of nature as one would do with a fine bottle of wine. There was something vibrant at the way the waves crashed on the beach and in the wind with its salty smell. He stood there and made a mental note to come back to Brighton after a decent interlude and spend more time here.

Later, back in his room he started to look at the address. He found a bus that would take him to the street where Darren lived. Greg got up early the next morning and took a bus to where Darren lived and waited. He sat down on a bench a short distance away pretending to read a newspaper yet still observing Darren's house. He didn't have to wait long. Darren, came out of his front door. Toast in one hand and his jacket draped over that arm as he tried to lock the door. He'd been to bed late and overslept but, yet he still had time.

Darren rushed to the bus stop but was unaware of the man in the dark jacket with a baseball cap surveying him as he made his way there. He got there just as the double decker bus stopped. Greg caught the bus and, instead of going to upper deck he sat on the bottom. He looked out of the bus as it drove along the route and saw Brighton at it's best and worst.

The many characters that had helped to make Brighton what it was. Still he wasn't there to judge the town but to follow orders and deal with the man who had, in the minds of the firm had made an attack on his country taking information that was meant to remain secret. The familiar 'Ting' as the request to stop brought Greg back to his mission. Darren came down the stairs looking to see of Tash was waiting for him as she normally had done every day since they had become an item.

He smiled as he saw her at the stop with two large takeaway cups of coffee in hand. Darren was always glad to see Tash. Greg knew that if it came to it she would have to be taken care of as well. Greg felt some sadness but, times before he'd had to take someone else out as well. He hoped not but in his line of work you could never tell. He followed them at a discreet distance, but he had reversed his jacket earlier just in case he'd been noticed.

Greg stopped at a coffee shop opposite the office. While he sipped his coffee, he surveyed the building. It was a typical office block built in the mid 70s and then it was the vogue but by now it was dated. The walls were grey and foreboding and didn't really inspire to want to go in unless, you had to. The building was about five floors. With a main double door and a reception desk to the left.

Greg got the mobile out of his trouser pocket and started to text. He pressed the send button and waited for a reply. When he did it was the name of a recruitment agency that dealt with Carewise. 'Kavanagh Select Choice Recruit'. He used the search engine to look for the agency. He got the address, finished his coffee and returned to his room. Tomorrow he'd register. That evening he sent a text before he got together the documents he needed. He slept, not knowing if he'd return to the nightmare of the war he'd fought in.

4

The next day he went to register at Kavanagh's. He stepped inside carefully and deliberately smiling at the bubbly talkative girl on the phone. He noticed her nameplate on the desk which said *Stacey Harris Consultant*. He'd seen and met hundreds of Staceys all over in his time, so he knew how to deal with them and with their bubbly personality which Greg knew was all an act but if it worked on who she needed to charm then why not?

"So, Matt, I'm reeeeeally desperate as my client said they'll close our contract if we don't get someone as soon as poss and I know I've always relied on you as our top worker…," she said to the person at the other end of the phone, knowing how to charm and flatter a person to get what she wanted.

"You can? Ooooooooh you're a star. Promise I'll make it up to you later luvvy. I'll send you everything by email byeeeeeeeeeeee!" knowing of course she'd somehow forget to make it up.

So long as she made the numbers for the week Stacey, would say anything to charm people and get them to do what she wanted. Greg gave her a warm smile as she gave a little wave. All an act but hey, business is business.

"Hi, my names Rob. I'm in England at the moment trying to find my ancestors and, was wondering about a job. I used to be in a call centre so, I know all about targets".

Not the targets he was really thinking of but something to impress anyone in recruitment.

"Well, sit down luvvy and I'll bring some forms for you to fill in. Can I bring you a drink while you're filling them out?" she asked.

"A coffee would be really great," smiling as he said that.

Her forced smile eased as she made her way to the kitchenette thinking that she could place him that would bring her up into second place. Greg didn't care about how well Stacey was doing all he was interested in was getting to Carewise, so he could be another step closer to his ultimate goal.

It didn't take long for Greg to complete the form. Eventually, Stacey came back with a company mug of coffee and sat down. She placed the mug on the company coaster and started to go through Greg's form.

"Mmmm, I see you've done call centre work in appliances. Hang on a mo luvvy I've just thought of something and I won't be too long," Stacey said as she went back to her desk.

Greg watched her at the other end of the office picking up her phone. Five minutes later she hurried back to Greg.

"Ooooo, aren't you the lucky one today, Rob!!" she said in her standard giggly office 'I'm so excited for you' way.

 "I can get you into Carewise on Monday," she said.

"Carewise?!" asked Greg pretending to be unaware of who they are.

"They do warranties on home appliances. I place lots of people there. and it's a reeeeally lovely company to work for," said Stacey in a very passionate manner.

Greg smiled. Success! He was in.

»What time on Monday?« he asked.

"If you arrive at nine, go to the reception desk and ask for Annie as she deals with the new starters," replied Stacey.

Ten minutes later Greg was on his way back to his room. First of all, he stopped at the coffee shop. Had a large cappuccino, sent a text to say that he'd got a job with the company that Darren worked for. A message came back to say good luck not that he needed any luck.

That night, Greg closed his eyes to the abyss of sleep. Once more, the sounds of Chalk 1 of the recon company being thrown into the cauldron of fire entered his mind, the war revisiting him like a vengeful ghost, the sounds of the planes screaming low the flashes, bangs and then…………...

The next morning, he went into town. Went around the computer shops and eventually bought the latest lap top and games. Greg didn't like games but felt if he was going to get close to his prey then, he had to show that he had some interest in computers and gaming to gain his trust. So, Monday morning he got ready. The Glock secure in his warm padded jacket. He got a couple of computing magazines and went to Carewise.

He opened the heavy glass door smiling, he walked to the desk in reception.

"Hi! My names Rob and I'm starting today," said Greg.

The receptionist looked up with her company smile.

"Ah yes, just take a seat and someone will be with you soon. If you just need anything my name's Annie," she said in a helpful friendly voice.

Greg sat down with the other new starters watching as the staff entered noisily as they talked about many things like how their teams were doing or, how a date went or what they were going to do on holiday. Greg just sat there and waited. He noticed Darren as he walked through the open doors with coffee in one hand and Tash's hand in the other. His eyes followed him with great interest trying to listen to what they were saying. It didn't really matter what they said as he knew he was another step closer. Shortly a young man with a black jacket fashionably torn dark grey jeans and a white t shirt with some punk rock art on it and his hair all slicked from hair gel trying to imitate Elvis. Looking every inch a rockstar spoke to them.

"Hi Guys! How're you all doing today? My names Brett and I'll be looking after you today. If you can grab your things just follow me," said Brett.

A sentence he'd repeated many times before. They walked through the doors to a room that was like a classroom with the layout of desks and computers.

"If you guys would like to sit at a desk and sort yourselves out, Martin, your trainer will be here soon, and he'll be training you. Anybody want a drink while you're waiting?" Brett said eagerly.

Some girls at the back were giggling to each other. A few people wanted drinks. Greg asked for a glass of water. Brett left the room with his mobile trying to text and walk at the same time. He came back with his tray just as Martin the trainer came in. After the drinks the training started. Greg was enjoying how Martin was doing the training. Martin knew the job and made people enjoy it mixing his experience and his unique sense of humour.

There was a lot to learn. How to use the system and the understanding of what the company was about. Sheets with questions at regular intervals to see how much they were picking up during the training session and so they could see how proficient they were becoming. At the lunch break. Greg sat in the rest room near where they were training and was starting to make a mental note of the building layout. The mental map of the building from what he had already seen was being completed in his mind. Where the entrances were, and the fire exits located. He'd have to wait till he got upstairs before seeing what the call floor was like.

That evening, he put the papers in order on the desk for the next morning. A few of the new starters were starting to make friends. He knew he'd have to make the odd friend as it might seem peculiar and more noticeable if he didn't.

"So, what did you think?" a new starter said to Greg.

"Oh, sorry, I was a million miles away. It was good. Enjoyed it!" Greg said as he forced a smile.

"My name's Jimmy. Yeah it wasn't bad. We'll see what it's like when we get up on the floor," Jimmy replied.

"Name's Rob, pleased to meet you, Jimmy," Greg replied.

"I'm going for a drink with some of the others. Do you want to along?" Jimmy asked.

"Thanks, but it's been a long day on the grey cells. How about some other time?" Greg said nicely but trying to concentrate on the job he was here for.

Greg walked home. He wasn't lying his head felt as though it was swimming. Coffee and a message back. Early night. He was dreading these moments of reliving the nightmare of that ambush in the desert. He could see his chalk's faces before they were flung into a stupid no logic mission. He'd love to meet one day those responsible for his chalk being decimated but, as Scarlett said in the film *Gone With The Wind,* »Tomorrow's another day«. He recalled the faces of the loved ones who had lost people from his unit at a private meeting being told some flag waving bullshit about how they died on a mission that was vital to the coalition forces and the successful outcome of the wider mission. Some of the partners and family hadn't swallowed the official line; others had reluctantly but Greg had been bound by an oath of secrecy and felt even more frustration about not being able to tell the truth that their loved ones had died because of dodgy intelligence.

The rapid breathing, the sweat, Greg woke up. Once more, Chalk 1 had bled. Once more Chalk 1 had seen the elephant.

Greg made his way back to Carewise in the morning with his magazines. He concentrated on the last day of training. Later after lunch on the next day they were going to the call floor to set up. Jimmy was chatting to some of the others. Greg waved at Jimmy who smiled and waved back at Greg. Later as they were upstairs and settling in he sat at his desk and looked at the pile of laminates which he started to arrange. Plugging in his headset and adjusting the volume. They started off with easy calls such as basic appointing of contractors. Despite everything, Greg was starting to get into the act. Greg saw where Darren was. He had to remain focused on his job. The mission. Time to go home. Greg started to pack up and put things in the lockers around the walls. Tomorrow he could see when Darren took his breaks and make sure that he was going on them at the same time.

Greg sat in the rest area giving the impression he was reading the games magazine hoping that Darren would take the bait. Darren walked in but wasn't noticing him. Still, he had to just bide his time. So, he had his sandwiches and like a good fisherman, he waited till his prey took the bait. It didn't take too long. Over a week later Greg was sitting reading his magazine.

"Hi!" Darren said, "Is this seat free?" as Darren couldn't find any other seats free that day.

"Oh, sure! Help yourself," Greg replied pretending to be surprised.

"I see you're reading GameComp. Really good magazine!" Darren said. "Heard of Zalon 2: infiltration? I'm playing that at the moment."

"Haven't got it, I'm sorry," Greg truthfully told him.

"Love gaming myself. Name's Rob!"

"Hi, Rob, I'm Darren," Darren told him in a friendly way as they shook hands.

"No problem. I can lend it to you at some point."

"That's kind of you, bro," Greg told him in a friendly way.

Darren and Greg spent the rest of the lunch break talking about computers and games Plus films and anything else. Over the next few days they were becoming friends. Greg started to like the guy and it was a shame that he would have to kill him, but he was a soldier and had to carry out the orders that he was given.

That evening Darren and Greg left the office together. It was there that Warren had been waiting for Darren, so they could go for a coffee. Warren noticed someone with Darren and for some reason, Warren had a sense of foreboding something troubling him but just couldn't put his finger on it. Warren had always been the type to worry about things. The sort of person who will worry about something tiny yet, could end up being a major worry. He'd known Darren for a long time ever since meeting him at a local computer fair nearly eighteen years previously. It was a chance meeting that sparked a great friendship.

Warren had been asking a question about a new hard drive when Darren had clumsily pushed through wanting to see what was going on and Warren had dropped a package which had his lunch in.

"Hey! What's up?" said Warren as he saw his lunch on the floor.

"Ah, my fault," Darren said realising what he'd done.

"Sorry, I didn't mean to bump into you," Darren said as he was helping Warren pick the remains of his lunch off the floor.

The computer rep was wiping remains of the meal off his shoes and wasn't happy about it.

"Sorry?! What about my lunch you div?!" Warren was getting stressed at this point.

Darren wasn't a bad guy but felt guilty at what he'd done.

"Look I'm sorry. My fault. I'll buy you something at the café," Darren told Warren. "I'm Darren."

"Warren! But people call me Wazza!" Warren said as his anger was subsiding.

"By the way, what did you think about the hard drive?" Darren asked him.

"Yeah, okay till my sandwiches went flying," Warren told him.

"Don't think the Rep was happy about the sandwich on his clean shoes!" Darren said to ease the tension.

Both of them had to admit it was pretty funny, which broke the ice as they went to get something to eat and that was the start of a life long friendship for the two lads. Warren had been the typical computer geek that always stood out in the crowd. He was a loner at school and out as Warren found it awkward to make friends. He liked computers as they were the only things that were never bad and treated him well unlike many of the bullys at school who pushed him around and called him names. "Oi, Four eyes, you daft git!" or the more common one was "Isn't the playground big enough for you bubble butt?" Warren took it painfully, the insults burning deep insidehim.

It was when Warren had started at the computer shop that he hit on the idea of getting back at Brendon, a lad around the same age as Warren who had a mission in life, and that was to make Warren's life as miserable as possible while getting the maximum pleasure from his deed. Warren had found out that Brendon was now working for a well-known finance company in Brighton. He was married to a beautiful wife and had two small children, but from what he heard, still had a mean streak inside him. He was also devoted to his car an Aston Martin DBS.

One day, he turned up at Brendon's office on the pretext that there was a fault with one of the servers. Warren conned his way inside to the office of his nemesis. Fortunately, Brendon didn't recognise as he'd been too busy tormenting some of his staff.

"Yes? What do you want?" Brendon said in a short way with a hint of malice in it.

"I've come to fix the fault with the DZ19A connector," Warren told him with a servile voice.

"Well, just don't make a mess!" Brendon said as he so wanted to vent his spleen on him, but as Warren was there as a 'guest' worker, he was unable to do so.

Not knowing what he was talking about Brendon sighed with reluctance and let Warren get on with whatever needed doing. Brendon left the room with the feel of someone who has a dark cloud following him about. Warren, happy that he could drop the grovelling flunky act could then get on with what he'd come to do. Minutes later the cover for the tower was off and Warren pulled from his bag a device – used mostly by the security services but available if you know the right contacts - that only a few people know of which was to link his computer with Bendons.

After fixing if, of course he took his time just to make Brendon angrier and more stressed he left the office with a carefree attitude just for effect he passed the staff room where a young secretary was in tears after meeting Brendon he knew that Karma would be a joy not only for him but, the people at the office. He passed reception the finish line he thought.

"Could you tell Mr James his PC is now ready?" Warren said with a touch of relief.

Warren got back to the shop and started to go into the Hard Drive of Brendon's computer. The tranasctions that Brendon was dealing with was just mind blowing. It was about the time when many office staff had left for the day that Warren noticed emails with 'exotic' titles like 'Headmasters meeting' from Saucy whiplash that he started to get interested in. He copied one of the addresses and started working on a plan. For the first time in his life, he was enjoying dealing with Brendon James. After he got an email back with a paid for receipt he got ready for the nextpart of his plan.

The trip to one of the dubious addresses in Brighton didn't take long the lady known as Mrs Cat Of Nine Whips beckoned him in. For what Warren was paying her she didn't care as long as her girls and business weren't going to suffer. He waited behind the double mirror video camera ready for the 'Star'. Warren, as it turned out didn't have long to wait as he heard the ladies give the usual talk to the client. For once, Brendon was calm and not aggressive. He entered the room wearing a crimson red basque with black stockings that had a red bow at the top. Warren could hear the script.

"You've been such a naughty boy, Headmistress will have to punish you!" said the girl as she started to whip him on the bottom.

Warren was thinking how this would be received by those who knew Brendon. He packed his camera away and gave the Madam twenty pounds as a tip. Warren then went back to the shop and started working. First the money from the company. Thirty thousand to Brendon's 'secret' account which he had set up on line. Eighty thousand to charity. Then, the best bit. He emailed the management team and after seeing and remembering the nametag of the young girl who was crying in the staffroom an email was sent to her as well All to gather in the conference room Monday morning at 10.30. Warren even made great care to put a note in Brendon's computer diary.

When Brendan saw the entry in the diary he was a little confused especially as it said finance, but he wanted to show how he was working hard and doing everything for the company. It was Monday and feeling amazingly proud of himself he was a Peacock gushing with self-importance and pride at his forthcoming performance as a 'star' employee.

 The meeting started off with a scowl for the young lady. What was she doing there? Brendon said to himself as he looked down his nose at her.

"Before we begin, Brendon," James Dillerton a member of the board spoke up slightly embarrassed and nervously. "We've come across a problem."

"A problem? I don't understand," Brendon said.

"We've found that there's over a hundred thousand missing," Dillerton said.

"No way! No Bloody way!" Brendon said. "I'm doing everything myself so its all accounted for." Brendan said as he always took the credit for the hard work his team put in as though he worked alone.

"I know we've had no issues before but a hundred and ten thousand is NOT small change." The Director of finance spoke as she looked at the spreadsheet.

"We had a tip, so we started to dig a little deeper, and we found thirty thousand in an account. Yours!"

Brendon was for once genuinely shocked. He was speechless, his world starting to crumble while cold sweat covered his body.

"That's not true! I haven't got thirty thousand in any account," he said.

The finance director slid the papers along the desk. Brendon picked them up. Was this an insane nightmare? A practical joke of sorts?

"We traced the balance to a charity called Huntingdon's which you deposited the balance. It would appear very badly in the public eye if we grabbed it back so Ken has made a statement to say that it's been a charity which we've always admired and wanted to make a donation that would really help their ongoing work."

By now Brendon was facing the end as he stood on the edge of a very very deep abyss. It was then the computer started the projector in a few minutes the entire board was watching Brendon's meeting with the 'Headmistress'. Heads looked speechless as this could do the company a lot of negative reviews if it ever got on various online sites. He was finished. Shortly after the Police took Brendon away for questioning. He lost all that he had. Home, car, job, friends but the worst that his wife took his children away and divorced him. By the time he got out of prison his wife had remarried and denied him custody of their children. Warren later read the news in the paper and felt relieved that he'd been able to do something about the person who had made his life hell.

He didn't worry about computers as when they went wrong as he had a natural ability to fix them. He soon started, but slowly, making friends that way. And one day started to experiment with hacking and by experience was getting very good at it. First, he would leave his 'tag' as graffiti artists do on buildings or bridges. But unlike the dangerous and illegal activity of physical tagging, Warren found this more fun. After a while, he would do things to help his granny whom he was staying with as he wanted to help her. He hacked into Brighton council and managed to lower her council tax.

After a couple of years, Warren found a job with a local computer shop which he really enjoyed. While he was there, he'd have access to the net be able to pick up snippets of information and be able to pick up items with staff discount for his passion of computing.

"New friend?" Warren asked.

"That's Rob over here from the states doing his 'I'm looking for my roots thing' and earning some cash in the meantime," Darren told his friend.

"Okay, hope you haven't told him anything," Warren said nervously.

"You think I'm that stupid? 'course not. Don't know him that well yet. As far as he knows, I'm a gaming fan," Darren replied as they walked to their favourite coffee bar.

A few days later, Darren was at Tash's for their evening together. Usually it went along the same way. A take away meal, bottle of wine watching a film followed by making love. They normally would take turns in choosing a film but, nearly every time it would be a romantic chick flick that Tash had wanted to see though she always said that Darren could choose the next time. Darren didn't mind, as long as Tash was happy then, he was happy. Normally they were relaxed as they sat in the candlelight. The flames from the candles dancing and casting shadows on the walls the soft scent that came from the candles filled the room though tonight was different as Darren wasn't really in the mood and seemed tense and edgy.

"Tash," Darren whispered into her ear.

"I DO!" she replied jokingly anticipating his formal proposal. "I need you to do something for me."

She gave Darren a coy smile.

"Naughty boy! We haven't finished the film yet," Tash said in a jokingly naughty hinting way.

"This is kinda serious, Tash," Darren replied firmly.

Tash started to get that worried feeling like a sense of doom as Darren had said it in that quiet serious way which she hadn't heard for a long time and was really out of character for Darren. She'd noticed that he hadn't been his normal relaxed self hardly touching his Tikka Massala all evening but seemed a little on edge and thought it could have been down to some bug.

"Is anything wrong hunny? Job? Ali? Us?"

"It's something more than that. I need you to look after something for me in case anything happens to me."

 Darren pulled out the memory stick and started to hand it to her.

"You daft bugger what have you done eh? Nicked the fucking crown jewels? Naughty holiday snaps?" Tash said in a teasing way.

"The less you know, babe, the better. Don't want you getting into deep trouble."

Tash was starting to get really spooked now. What was going on? What's he saying? She thought. Something wasn't right, and Tash could sense something. She started to get angry.

"I want to fucking know! I'm your woman. What happens, happens to both of us. We're a fucking partnership not joined at the hip, but a fucking team like Batman and Robin, The Lone Ranger and that Indian what's his name bloke."

"Tonto." Darren corrected her.

He knew she hated that, but it was a way of changing the subject to make her stop still and focus on a different subject.

"You going to stop that?!"

"Stop what?"

"Always bloody correcting me, Mr Darren 'I bloody know it all' Radcliffe."

By now she was starting to cry. Darren pulled her closer to him. Realising he could have done this a bit better if he had waited and told her when he hadn't been so stressed. Darren thought she was right though. This had been playing on his mind. Maybe he'd been a fool to do this but then at the time it had seemed so thrilling, the dare and risk had made things so exciting. If he was married, he wouldn't need to go online and hack places. Tash would be a good motive to be more stable and responsible as he knew and had known for a long time that they would make a good married couple.

"Tash?"

"What is it? Want me to look after your bloody sheep now?"

"No." he laughed at that."

"What then?"

"Will you marry me?"

He pulled the ring box from his jacket pocket and her smudged face from her tears that had made her make up run lit up in the flickering candlelight when she saw the ring. She looked up at him smiling.

"Of course, you daft bugger." She kissed him passionately on the lips. "Though, it'll cost you."

"Another take out?" Darren asked in a playful way.

She playfully punched him.

"How about a new pair of shoes, you silly sod?!" she said changing the sadness into laughter.

They both laughed. Quickly embraced and kissed. She quickly took the stick and hid it behind some books though not well-hidden and rushed back to make love with Darren.

Much later, she left a voicemail message for her parents.

"Mum, Dad, it's Tash. Mum, I Know you're both asleep at the moment, but just quickly wanted to say that I think you should go out and buy yourself a hat. Why? Just that Darren's asked me to marry him and of course I said YEEEEESSSSSSS!!!! Just that I'm on cloud nine at the mo. Speak to you guys later byeeeeeeeeeeeeeee."

She put the phone down. She was so so so much on the cloud nine and the happiest person in the world. Now, she thought let's start planning the wedding. She laid down in the bed and cuddled up to Darren who was by now sound asleep. My Man she thought as she drifted off to sleep with her arm draped over him with the happiest smile she'd ever had. Tash had even already started thinking of dresses.

5

The next day was a special day at the office as they officially announced their engagement to their friends. The girly shrieks as Tash showed off her ring to all her girlfriends. Then the hugs and handshakes from everyone. And as the day progressed banners, cards and all sorts of special confetti found their way on the floor, and the pings as texts came in to their phones with congratulations. Normally, this was frowned on, but on special days like these, management often turned a blind eye.

"Congrats, big fella!" said Ali, beaming with a huge smile beneath his greying beard rushing up to congratulate both Darren and Tash with a firm handshake and hug.

"Let's hope it's going to get the figures up," he said seriously yet light-heartedly though hinting that while it was a special day for them, the official business was still business.

Darren had a feeling that he hadn't had such a feeling for a long time. That things were now starting to look on the way up and were going to be better as a married man especially when his partner was Tash, he could find the responsibility he'd been looking for, and maybe there could be kids one day soon. Hoping that their children wouldn't need to be as silly with computers as he'd been. If only his parents were still around then, that would have been better for them to see how he turned out. Not the dodgy work on the computer but how he'd done well at work and, being lucky enough to settle down at last with a lovely lady like Tash.

A few days later in the evening Ms Jo Sikorska, a retired lady of Polish descent who lived opposite Darren 'noticed' a figure near the street lamp outside her home. She was a lady who liked things to be ordered and secure, as her late father had taught her since choosing to live in England coming like many Poles to escape from their country which had been overrun by the Germans and wanted to fight alongside Britain in her hour of need and help liberate their country, and rather than return to Poland now occupied by the 'liberating' Russians, decided to remain and become part of a country, whose values and way of life he admired; he felt that Britain would be the ideal country to settle down and raise a family in.

Her father, Michal, had opened a small chain of hardware stores the sort where you got what you wanted no matter how little you needed. After his death, Jo, despite having gone to university had taken over the family business which she had run almost single-handedly making it a success as her father would have wanted.

After she retired, she passed the business over to her sons. She had been born in Brighton but was proud of her Polish roots. After getting divorced as a result of her husband's drunken and abusive behaviour, she decided to revert to her Polish maiden name. That evening, Ms Sikorska had noticed a figure standing near her home looking suspiciously at Darren's house through the gap in her living room curtains and, as a part of her civic duty had called the Police.

Greg had visited Darren before, and on that occasion had met his neighbour on the way to Darren's front door. This time he decided to look round to see if there was anyone watching, but this time didn't see anybody, not realising that serious eyes were watching him securely from behind closed curtains nearby.

He stepped up to Darren's front door and used the knocker a couple of times looking through the frosted glass panels to see if Darren was coming as it was getting cold. Waiting for Darren to open the door, he checked in his jacket and felt the reassuring presence of the Glock. He'd checked it earlier. It worked and was loaded. This time he was going ahead; he couldn't wait anymore. Darren greeted Greg at the door with a smile.

"Hi, Dude! Come on in!" Darren said as Greg stepped into the warm comfy sanctuary of his house.

"Thanks, Darren," Greg replied.

They both went into the living room. Consoles on the table ready to play the new game which Darren had told Greg about.

"Coffee?" Darren asked.

"You read my mind, Bro," Greg said as he tried to warm up a little.

"Make yourself at home."

"Sure will!" Greg said happily.

As soon as Darren had gone to make the drinks, Greg started to go through what was on Darren's desk. Disks and papers. Greg had been trained in the latest aspects of cyber dealings and recognised some of the names written on the rewrite disks that people made copies with.

"Hey Rob, would you like…… What you up to man?" Darren said, shocked as he returned to the living room to ask Greg something and saw Greg rifling through the papers and discs strewn on his desk.

"Rob, what the fuck are you up to?" Darren repeated surprised and shocked at this intrusion into his private things.

"Where's the information?"

Greg dropped the laid-back American style and became the professional intelligence officer he was.

"What you talking about? You crazy on drugs? Think you'd better go, mate."

Darren was getting rattled by what Greg was doing.

"Not until I get the information."

"Really haven't got a clue what you mean."

"Let me refresh your memory. A short time ago, you hacked into a site of interest to my country. You were good, but we managed to trace you and the time and date it happened. The last time I was here I found a disk you made of an app called Kryptozogol, which is a system used by hackers. Then, you said that you've got a copy of Team Zalon 2: infiltration. I checked, and that's still in the Beta stage and not yet released. So, what have you got to say?"

"So, someone gave me a copy of a dodgy game! So fucking what? Is this what it's about? That I've a bootleg game?"

"Don't think I was born yesterday! Do you think I'd be here just for a dumb game?" Greg said in an angry voice.

Greg pulled out his Glock from its warm, secure place in his jacket to reinforce his point. The sight of it made Darren shake with fear. He'd never been threatened in his home before let alone by someone with a gun or had seen a real gun that closes. A single bead of sweat from fear made its slow journey down the side of Darren's face. Greg slowly turned the safety from safe to live.

"A ciggy lighter?"

Darren tried to ease the tension with some humour, worried that this time he was so well in over his head and he wasn't going to get out of this too easily or even at all.

"Don't play dumb and fuck with me!"

Greg was starting to get irritated with Darren's behaviour. "Do you really think if this was a ciggy lighter that I'd be able to do this?"

Greg, to make his point, slowly pulled the barrel back with the sound of a round being chambered making the message very clear. Very clear to Darren indeed.

"So, just stop playing games and give me the information you got and don't pretend I'm some dumb fucking Yank backpacker doing the Europe thing!" said Greg, almost shouting at Darren.

Darren was thinking fast trying to buy time, but what use if he did? If he didn't give him the information Greg would shoot him just as surely, he'd still shoot him if he did. Still to think and play for time and hope beyond hope that a miracle would happen. If only he hadn't taken that tip what a fool he'd been and now he was paying for it.

Greg started to slowly step back aiming the gun all the time at Darren and not noticing that Darren's cat was there and suddenly, the cat made a screeching noise as Greg stood on its tail. Greg was distracted and confused losing his balance started to fall and would have fallen hard on the floor had it not been for the computer table. His hand landed on the table as Darren started to rush him. Greg fired his gun missing Darren, and the bullet that had been meant for Darren went through the window. With Darren almost on him in anger, Greg fired again, and this time the bullet didn't miss but went through Darren's head showering the wall and curtains in blood, bone and pieces of brain.

The room seemed eerily quiet. Time, for that instant, had frozen. Momentarily Greg was taken back to an earlier time while the smoke from his gun danced in the light in some form of a macabre ballet. Greg quickly composed himself taking stock of the situation and thinking fast as he'd been trained to do.

The sound of the Police banging at the door brought him back to his training. Looking round he saw that the back window was unlocked very quickly he turned the handle opened the window and left the house. By now, only the cat, sitting on the stairs as though defending its home was left alive in the house.

6

Constables Nik Orr and Paul Jenkinson had parked their car outside in response to call about someone hanging around suspiciously and were now talking to Ms Sikorska who lived opposite Darren and was worried she'd seen a Peeping Tom. Nik took his new style Police baseball hat and put it on his head. Nik was one of many officers who would rather wear either the traditional helmet or, the peaked hat rather than the new hat. But, it was the new style which had been enforced on many officers by those higher up.

Nik walked up to the front door took out his warrant card knocked on the door and waited for Ms Sikorska to open the door.

"Hello, Ms Sikorska? Evening. I'm PC Nik Orr, and this is my colleague PC Paul Jenkinson," Nik said introducing himself as he showed her his warrant card.

"So, Ms Sikorska, in your own words, can you try and give me a description of what he looked like?" asked Nik as he was trying to write down what Ms Sikorska was saying in the near dark with only the hall light to aid him.

Paul was looking around the immediate area with his torch trying to see if there was anything he could find. Nik and Paul had both known each other ever since they had been in the army together and after their discharge, they both wanted to join the Police. They'd been on the Brighton force now for eight years and loved working in the town.

"It was a bit difficult as I only saw him for a few minutes; and saw him standing under the street lamp there. I'm sure he's been here before. I could swear I've seen him around here before. He was about your colleague's height; I think he had a beard. I know he was wearing a dark jacket, and one of those baseball caps," she said, trying to be helpful.

THWACK. The sound of the bullet striking the wall sending down a shower of brick and plaster on the three of them, made all three jump, as PC Orr was taking down the description. They sprinted across the road. Paul grabbed his Airwaves radio.

"Shots fired 62 Henderson Road. Urgent assistance required," he said as they ran across the road to the scene.

Knowing that shortly they'd get the back up of any available units nearby, but for now, they only had each other, Nik nervously reached for the door, but it was locked. He looked in through a gap of the curtains and seeing Darren's lifeless body on the floor he decided to go in. Banging on the door.

"Police! Open up!" he said firmly.

They waited a bit. Still nothing.

"Smash the glass," said Paul, as he was reaching for his baton.

Though if the person who had shot Darren was still there what good was a baton or spray?

"Ok, be ready on three."

They both counted down to three which seemed like an eternity. Paul had his baton at the ready. Nik smashed a hole with his baton, elbowed the broken glass and reached in and opened the door.

They entered. Quiet was all they heard. The back window was open. The back curtains were slowly moving in the breeze from outside. Greg had already left the property as soon as he'd heard the Police and was following what he'd been trained to do in the art of evasion. Hiding close by in some bushes he waited for the right moment to leave. Nik and Paul both looked round the room and saw only Darren's lifeless body lying in a pool of blood on the living room floor the blood following the joins of the laminate flooring. Careful not to enter or disturb anything they followed procedure and called it in.

"Officer 603 62 Henderson Road. Fatal shooting. Require an ambulance."

Paul said into his handset. Seeing Darren's cat waiting on the stairs for the owner that would no longer look after him they could but only wait.

DCI Jarrod Fischer had finally just drifted off into sleep as the mobile on his bedside cabinet woke him up. He slowly reached for the ringing mobile hoping it wasn't his ex-wife complaining again that she didn't get her alimony or that it wasn't enough. He was relieved when he saw that it was his deputy Peter calling.

Jarrod had been a Police officer all his life. It was something that he'd wanted to do since he was a boy as his father had been a sergeant on the Brighton force and one of his joys as a child was to meet his dad while he was on the beat. Wearing his clothes and the toy Police helmet he felt every inch an officer and had become the junior mascot of his dad's station. Years later after his exams, he'd applied and done his training at Hendon College. After the hard work, he graduated not quite getting the baton of honour but just happy that his dad was proud of him. Jarrod had often dismayed his father by being a bookworm. He'd got an A in his English 'A' levels and would often carry a copy of poems while he was a rookie police officer. Jarrod had risen quickly through the ranks. In his late 20s, he married Sarah but divorced seven years later as she could not compete with his other love the Police Force. She was always on at Jarrod that the alimony wasn't enough despite living with a much older man whom she had met on social media.

Jarrod remembered all too well that evening after he'd just been accepted for an interview to become a detective. He'd been to a travel agency and was thinking about going to Seychelles with Sarah just as his interview to go forward for Detective training had been approved and what better way to start it off by going somewhere special with his wife, Sarah. He had brought the magazines with him as he entered the front door.

"I'm home!" Jarrod had said excitedly said as he hurried inside looking forward to them sitting down together to choose their dream holiday package.

"I'm up here, Jarrod," Sarah said.

Jarrod made his way upstairs with magazines in his hands excited to show Sarah about a great holiday just before he would have his interview.

"I've got something I'd like to show you," Jarrod said as he entered the bedroom.

He couldn't believe his eyes as Sarah was packing a suitcase. He froze as she seemed to be indifferent.

"What's all this, love?" Jarrod asked in a confused and scared moment as the holiday went out of his mind now it no longer seemed the number one item on his agenda.

"Sit down, Jarrod. I need to talk with you," Sarah told him.

Jarrod tried to sit near Sarah, but she wanted some distance and intentionally made a deliberate gap between them.

"Jarrod, I'm not going to beat around the bush. I'm leaving," Sarah told Jarrod.

It was at his point that Jarrod's world collapsed. The shock of what Sarah had said and seen what she was doing made him go weak. The elation of coming home and the thought of them talking about the holiday of a lifetime, then Sarah's revelation burst his bubble just like that without any thought how he would take it.

"Why?" Jarrod asked.

"I can't compete with your other love, Jarrod," she said.

"I just can't do it anymore!"

"I'm not seeing anyone else!" Jarrod told her truthfully.

"I'm not talking about another woman, but that would be easier in a way. I'm talking about the Force," she said emotionally.

"I'll resign and find another job, Sarah," Jarrod told her.

"Oh yes, you would. I know you'd find something else more routine. The normal hours the security and being out of danger. God knows, Jarrod, how I would lie awake at nights wondering if you'd come home. Frightened if some crazed person hadn't harmed you and I'd have you to myself in the evenings. But, in six months, or a year you'd realise how you'd hate it about having resigned from the Police. There would be a tiny piece of you that would feel anger and resentment towards me for taking you away from your job. Jarrod, I know you'd never blame me directly, but there would be a tiny piece in you which would say 'it's my fault'. Some women can cope and adapt but I can't. I know you're gutted and churned up inside about this, but you're a good man, Jarrod. The Police needs men like you. Maybe there's a woman that knows the life and would want to be with you despite being in the police. I'm so so sorry that I'm not the woman for you," she said as tears started to fall from her eyes. Jarrod was confused at what she was saying, trying to absorb and analyse what she was saying. He was on the verge of starting to cry and would have done so had it not been for the distraction of the door opening and steps quickly coming up the stairs.

"Hi Hunny!" the voice said. "How're you dar......? Aah!" as Sarah and Jarrod saw Gordon enter the bedroom.

"Hello, mate," Gordon said to Jarrod as he held out his hand.

Jarrod stood there looking at Gordon's hand hanging as though like a puppet waiting for a string to make it move. Jarrod brushed past Gordon and walked down the stairs. Gordon looked at Sarah as if to say what's up with him? As he left the house, Sarah came after him and stopped him halfway down the path.

"How long?" asked Jarrod.

"About five months," Sarah said unhappily.

"So, for five months you've been sleeping with him?" Jarrod said.

"There's no need for that tone!" Sarah was getting angry with Jarrod.

"What sort of tone do you expect?" Jarod was getting angry now.

"One with a bit of respect for a start!!" Sarah demanded.

"I'm supposed to show a bit of respect for some Loads of Money-type who's been sleeping with my wife?" Jarrod replied.

"It's up to you but yes!" Sarah insisted.

Jarrod returned to the house, so he could get a few things. He could hardly believe what he had just heard. Show some respect? Why? As he was packing, he could hear them talking in the kitchen. He packed a large bag.

"I'll be back at some point to collect the rest of my things. I'll let you know when, so it doesn't inconvenience you," he told Sarah.

"Catch you later, mate!" Gordon said from the kitchen.

Jarrod left without saying anything to him. He realised that Gordon was the type to make something out of it if he answered back. Being a Policeman, he knew he had to have mental discipline in the face of this. He drove to his parents and waited to compose himself before going to the door with a bag and who was surprised to see him standing there on their doorstep.

"What's up son?" his dad asked. "Kicked you out?"

"No. I left. I'll tell you more inside. Can I come in and I might need a bed for a few nights till I get myself sorted out," Jarrod said to his dad.

His dad had been always a good father who wouldn't have it any other way. The shock on his wife's face as she saw her son put a bag on the floor near the front door.

Jarrod sat down in the living room while his parents sat there listening. They were stunned by the news that their son's marriage had broken down and Jarrod explained all that had happened that night with him finding out that Sarah had been cheating under his nose for the last five months. How he'd been looking forward to arranging a holiday with Sarah only to find her lover enter the house as they were there. He sat back in the armchair feeling relieved at having gotten it all off his chest. Feeling calmer now not the tense shaking person he was when he arrived outside their house.

Jarrod eventually found a flat, and weeks later; he found out that Gordon and Sarah had split up. He wasn't sorry. Not long after Sarah had met someone else through Social Media if that's what she wants to make herself happy then, so be it, Jarrod said to himself at the time. Jarrod was to rise quite quickly through the detective ranks eventually to become DCI.

"Pete, what are you doing up at this late hour?" Jarrod said as he tried to force himself more awake rubbing his eye while looking at the clock and hoping that Pete had just accidentally called him by mistake as he looked at the clock on the bedside cabinet.

"Sorry, boss, but there's been a shooting, and I think you need to have a look at this," Peter told Jarrod.

Jarrod looked at the clock and sighed when he saw what time it was but knowing he was a professional who expected others to have the same standards he had taken down the details, then had a shower before getting dressed. Forty minutes later, he was at the scene.

The flashing lights of the police cars and the mortuary vehicle bathed in blue flashing lights told him it was going to be the start of a long night for him. He could see the police in their dayglow vests making sure that people were kept back from looking at the scene.

Peter greeted his boss and gave him a cup of coffee. Jarrod savoured the caffeine hit as he stepped inside the house while those who were allowed in the living room were getting on with the task in hand dressed in their protective clothing designed to prevent contamination of a crime scene. He poked his head inside as the coroner's team were starting to take the body away. Jarrod refrained from looking at Darren as he knew he'd get a chance at the mortuary.

"Age 34. Name Darren Radcliffe. He worked at Carewise appliances as it says on his ID. We've let RSPCA know that there is a cat here, so they can try and rehome it," Peter said.
Jarrod took the bag with the ID. He made up his mind to speak to the people Darren had worked with at Carewise in the morning. It wasn't really his job but, in some ways, he felt it helped as it gave him a chance to put together a picture of the deceased and why someone would have killed him.

"Thanks, Pete. Make sure you get a report on this and from the officers who called this in as soon as you can."

 By now the mortuary team were putting Darren's body in the van and taking him to the mortuary fora postmortem. Jarrod then left for his flat. He undressed again, climbed into bed and fell into a deserved sleep.

By this time, Greg had arrived back at his room. To anyone else who saw Greg, it would have seemed that Greg had been out clubbing in Brighton and had come back to the flat a little worse for wear. He washed and got in bed. He'd done part of the job, but where was the information? This was going to play on his mind. He'd send a message later to keep the controller up to date with what was happening. Later that morning, Jarrod woke. He dressed again and made his way to Carewise before heading into the office. He joined the workers as they entered the door like a never-ending worm of humanity some noisy as they discussed many things of the night before or how their football teams were doing or a didn't care attitude towards being at Carewise.

"Good morning," Jarrod said to the receptionist who jumped in surprise as she was trying to finish off her coffee and pastry. The receptionist smiled as she wiped her mouth. Jarrod knew why he was there and tried to smile back as best as he could considering the circumstances.

"How can I help?" Michelle said.

"I need to speak with the person in charge of the building," Jarrod said.

"That's Mike Jones. I'll just see if he's free. Who shall I say is here?" asked Michelle.

"DCI Jarrod Fischer," Jarrod replied.

A few eyes turned towards Jarrod as he said that. Some of the workforces were curious why a police officer was there, and others started to feel uncomfortable as they thought he was there to see them. Some of them had heard of him due to having dubious encounters with the Police. Jarrod sat on the well-worn dark brown leather sofa opposite reception and waited.

"Hi!" Michelle said as she caught Jarrod's attention.

"Mike said he'll be down in a few minutes. Is there anything I can get you while you're waiting?" she asked.

Jarrod politely declined her offer. It was at this moment that Greg walked through the doors catching sight of Jarrod. He could recognise a Police officer anywhere without any trouble how they always stood out. He walked past. Just ignore him Greg told himself If they had come to arrest him there would be more of them. Was his first thought.
Very soon the imposing figure of Mike Jones, the larger than life boss of Carewise, made his way down to reception. He greeted Jarrod.

"I'm Mike Jones, the boss here. I understand it's not a business or social matter the reason that you've dropped by?" Mike asked curiously as he finished shaking his hand.

"I'd rather not say here. Is there somewhere a bit more private we can go?" Jarrod said quietly.

"If you'd like to follow me, Inspector."

Jarrod followed Mike as he went through the double doors to the ground floor where the offices and training rooms were located. Mike was still curious why Jarrod would want to go to a discreet room. He opened the glass door to one of the meeting rooms. They sat down at a table. Jarrod felt a little bit more at home here.

"I understand that you have an employee by the name of Darren Radcliffe?"

Jarrod began in the way he'd done many times before.

"Yes, he's one of the leading members of Ali's team, in fact, he's Ali's deputy. Is there a problem?" Mike said as alarm bells started to ring in his head.

"In that case," Jarrod went on, "could you ask Ali to join us?"

"Of course, He's in today. If you hang on, I'll get him," Mike said as he picked up the handset on the desk. Pressing the buttons to call Ali, Mike was making a mental note to ask Facilities to improve the cleanliness in the building as the phone he picked up was not all that clean.

"Hi, Ali!" Mike said, "Could you pop down now to training room A1 for me? As there's someone here who wants to talk to us about Darren."

"He'll be down shortly, Inspector," Mike said.

A few minutes later, Ali came in the room in his usual relaxed manner. Mike was looking serious, so Ali wondered why and who the visitor was.

"Ali, I'd like to introduce you to DCI Fischer of Brighton Police. He'd like a few words about Darren," Mike told Ali.

"What's he done? Bit of drunk and disorderly?" Ali joked.

"I'm afraid that I've some bad news, gentlemen. Last night Darren Radcliffe was found dead at his home. I can't go into any details at the moment, but was he close to anyone here? Do you know about family and friends?" Jarrod said.

Both men sat in silence. Shocked and numbed. The news that Darren, one of the members of Ali's team had been killed was a shock and they were trying to let it sink in. Only a couple of days ago Darren had helped in setting up a new incentive for the team which had started to prove popular and rewarding. Ali was shaking his head in disbelief. Mike was just as affected by the news.

"There's Tash," Mike said after a moment of silence.

"Tash?" Jarrod asked.

"Yes, she's or, shall I say his. Sorry, was his fiancée," Ali tried to speak but the shock of what he'd been told had thrown him into a state of confusion. "And no, he didn't have any family that I know of, at least he didn't mention any family members."

Jarrod tried to imagine how they were going to break the news. It's never easy to break the news about the death of someone that's known and well liked despite all the training, but it's a job that must be done at some point. Ali tried to find the words in his mind. He knew he could brief Tash's friends to be there as he broke the news to her while Mike would then switch the phones off so that the office could be told. He hoped that Tash would have someone with her when she went to see Darren at the chapel of rest. Jarrod made his way to his office. It was a relief to get into the fresh air. Later that afternoon there was a knock on Jarrod's office door. It was Pete.

"Come."

"Hi! Is it okay?" Peter asked as he put his head round the door.

"Of course. What have you got for me?" Jarrod asked hopefully.

"Well, we've got the reports back from forensics. Rather strange, really."

"Strange? Now, that's a surprise," Jarrod said lightly, "Tell me."

"Well, apart from the deceased's prints we came across a set belonging to Natasha Jones. She was questioned a few years ago on a breach of the peace, and we took her prints as a matter of precaution. Then, we found another set. Quite fresh. We couldn't trace the prints on the system, so I tried to trace on the European Databases. Again, we drew a blank. A wild shot I know but, we even managed to get access to our Israeli friends. We'd found that there was a lot of computing equipment and magazines suggesting that the deceased was into computing in a big way. We're getting his computer looked at in case there's anything that can give us a bit more information on the deceased."

Jarrod's eyes opened in wonder at how Peter was doing. He liked how his protégé was doing and thinking outside the box. The chance, though a long shot, was possible that somehow the deceased had managed to upset the Israelis. Not a good thing to have a Mossad freelancer running loose and unchecked about the city.

"But we even drew a blank from the Israelis. However, one avenue remained open. I have a friend in the U.S.; he's a police officer in Detroit, and I sent him a copy of the prints, and this is where it scored." Peter said positively.

Jarrod sat up. Now, Pete suddenly had Jarrod's undivided attention.

"So, what does it say about the suspect?"

"He's dead." Peter answered.

"The suspects dead?" Jarrod was getting confused.

We've a victim. Now a suspect who's dead. Ghosts killing people. Peter's been watching too much TV.

"Here's the report on the suspect. As you can see it's pretty interesting."

Jarrod looked down at it. To say it was impressive was putting it mildly. Sergeant Major Gregory Cochrane. Second Recon battalion Bravo company which was attached to the U.S. Special Forces. Been to all the major bases for training in the states. Forts Benning, Bragg and Lejeune. The second Gulf War in Iraq. A photo of a man in fatigues and beret looking into the camera heading the page.

"We also retrieved the bullet. Not an ordinary one. More likely used with a Glock," Peter said.

"There's just one more thing," Peter said in his 'I'm saving the best bit to last' voice.

Jarrod studied the object in the evidence bag.

"We found this memory stick taped to the back of a cabinet in the living room," he said as he put the bag and its content on Jarrod's desk.

"It's been tested for prints, so it's okay to look at," Peter said.

Peter left the room while Jarrod went over the details of the 'dead' soldier's history again. Even a stint with Charlie

Beckworth's Delta Force. Silver Star, Bronze Star, Purple Heart; this guy had the stuff. The suspect had been the equivalent of a warrant officer in the British Army but was killed when his chopper had gone down following an extraction after a mission during Operation Iraq Freedom. No details of the mission he was on obviously the details of the mission are still secret. He looked at the innocent looking device still in the clear plastic bag. Stared at it. Thought to himself. Is it for this that you were murdered? He reached for the stick on his desk. He took it out and inserted it into the USB slot of his laptop. A Screen came up showing a page of a newspaper with an empty field. Jarrod tried to type in a few characters but nothing except skull and crossbones that laughed at him. It seemed to Jarrod that in a way Darren was trying to taunt him even after death.

"You're not making this easy, are you?" he said to the memory stick.

Jarrod sat at his desk, leaned back in his chair and feeling frustrated as he turned the stick over and over and over between his thumb and forefinger.
"You're making this difficult for me. What are you saying to me? Why were you taped to the back of a cabinet?" he said to the memory stick.

He put the device back in its bag, took it to the evidence room and went home.

7

The next morning, instead of going straight to his office Jarrod decided to get a coffee at one of the mobile burger sites around the town, and as a way of trying to help, treated himself had a bacon and egg sandwich. Jarrod took off his dark beanie hat and put it into the pocket of his jacket. Realising that he hadn't shaved, he sat down ready for the coffee to wake him up a bit.

"Bit of a change today, chief!" said Matt, wiping some knives clean that he'd been using to make filled French sticks he owned the bar.

He took over the family-run business from his father and over years, had made a success of his services. After school, Matt would rushed home to help his dad prepare for the next day. Each night he'd be late to bed as his dad had insisted he did his homework as well. Matt had spent his Saturday mornings working with his dad in the burger van before going to watch Brighton at the old Goldstone ground. Jarrod enjoyed having a coffee at Matt's more than at the canteen. He could think too, rather than having the distraction of the canteen at work and even his office. He could sit and think and not worry about being disturbed. He enjoyed chatting with Matt talking about many things especially football and setting the world to rights.

"It feels great to have one of these sandwiches with a coffee," Jarrod said as he savoured every bite he took despite it not being healthy. But who cares? It wasn't every day.

»Up to much tonight?« Matt asked.

"Going home flicking through the channels eating a ready-made meal maybe a cold drink and then that's it, off to bed. What about you, Matt?"

"Tonight, the other half wants to watch one of those Hitchcock films."

Hitchcock thought Jarrod. He should have worked for the police. In the films, the bad guys always lost. Things might have been easier.

"Oh, which one?"

"The one with that posh English guy. You know, Cary Grant, otherwise known as Archie Leach who was born in Bristol."

Matt was a constant source of film trivia. One of those guys who'd you would like on a pub quiz team as they have all the answers to those movie questions that no one else knows. To Jarrod, it was as if Matt had written the book on film trivia.

"It's the one where he's a retired thief in France. *To Catch A Thief* – that's it, that's the name of the film. 'bout how a thief catches a thief."

It was at that moment that Jarrod had the Eureka moment. Of course, how could he have been so thoughtless! His mind had started to think about something — a course of action and hope.

"Matt, you're a genius," Jarrod said as he got up, paid and walked to the office feeling a bit better.

Matt was surprised. Genius? Over the years he'd been called a lot of things, some funny, others were not so pleasant, but to be a called a genius was a nice surprise. He smiled to himself as he carried on preparing the food for the customers that would come later and amusing himself about putting the word genius on his burger van. "Matt 'The Genius' Melville's burger bar" of course with the seagull, showing he was a passionate Brighton supporter, it had a nice touch he thought to himself.

Jarrod returned to his office. He smiled at his PA as he walked past her desk. He drew up a plan in his mind. But he'd made a slight detour to collect a form from the stationary cupboard on the way. As usual, it was locked. Despite being a police station if it hadn't had been locked, then there would be just an empty cupboard left by the end of the day.

"Mary, can I have something from the cupboard, please?" he asked the lady sitting next to it.

"Of course, you can," she said as helpful as ever. "What do you need?"

"Just an Official Secrets Act form," Jarrod replied.

Without asking why, Mary reached in and pulled out an updated copy. She put it in an envelope and handed it to Jarrod.

As soon as Jarrod had got to his office, he sat down without even taking off his jacket and started dialling.

"Hello, Lewes Prison. Good Morning! It's DCI Fischer. I need to speak with a prisoner by the name of Eddie Mahon tomorrow at half ten. Can I see him in an interview room please? You can? That's great," he said as Jarrod ended the call.

He sat back in his chair. He put the plastic bag with the stick on his desk, which he'd collected from the evidence room put it in front of him and smiled at it.

"Very soon, my little friend, we'll see what you've got to say!" Jarrod then sent his PA an email to block out his diary for the next morning.

The next day Jarrod drove directly to Lewes prison after stopping off a newsagent for a packet of cigarettes and a paper. It was an imposing structure on the outskirts of Lewes. Built in the early 1850s, it now had over 700 inmates, and at one time had hosted the likes of Reggie Kray Ronnie's less known but more dangerous twin. He parked the car, made his way through the gates and proceeded to the interview room, where Eddie was nervously sitting drinking a coffee while he waited. A prison officer was standing behind him nodded and left as Jarrod walked in.

"Hello, Mr Fischer," Eddie said sitting relaxing in his chair as Jarrod entered.

"How're you keeping, Eddie?" Jarrod asked.

Eddie wasn't a bad person but had just been unlucky in life. He had worked hard for a local company and kept his nose clean but had been unfairly laid off in order to save money on redundancy payments; this he had taken badly and so had decided to seek his own form of justice by causing problems on the firm's computer system and managed to transfer twenty thousand into his own account before Jarrod and the Police caught him. Jarrod himself had had to arrest him; with a sense of unhappiness not that he condoned in the action and the theft of money, but the way the firm had treated Eddie in the first place was almost a crime. His wife Suzy saw Eddie as he was being led down and shouted at him.

"We'll be waiting for you! Just keep your nose clean, Eddie!" she said as he turned to look at her fleetingly as he disappeared into the bowels of court before he was taken away to start his sentence.

"I'm doing well, but I'm worried about Suzy and little Jimmy, how they're doing. It's just that Suzy says everything's okay, but she does hide a lot, so I do worry, Mr Fischer," Eddie replied. "How can I help you?"

"I need some help with a memory stick that's got an unusual log in so proving difficult to get through to find out what's on it," Jarrod said.

Jarrod passed the cigarettes and paper across the table towards Eddie, who gratefully accepted them.

"Eddie, I'm not going to give you any fancy talk or, make any promises I can't keep but what I will say is, help me and I'll see what I can do to help your wife and son by getting Social services to see them so that they can help to find out what they need," Jarrod told Eddie.

Eddie took in what Jarrod had to say. He had treated Eddie very fairly, and in return, Eddie had helped Jarrod with the investigation by being fully cooperative, so the court had been as lenient as possible with his sentence.

"Before we go any further, I need you to read and sign this." Jarrod took the envelope with the form from inside his jacket and passed it along the table to Eddie.

Eddie slowly opened it and unfolded the form; his eyes opened wide in surprise.

»What's going on, Mr Fischer?« Eddie asked nervously.

"I can only tell you at this moment what I have. I know it's only a little, but until you agree and sign then I can't tell you anything else," Jarrod said.

"What about my family?"

"They're okay as they know nothing."

"I don't want to ruin my chances of getting out and somehow starting afresh. I 'm doing some classes in tiling and it's looking good."

Eddie was getting optimistic. Eddie thought for a few seconds, and then gestured for a pen. Jarrod took one from his jacket and passed it to him, and Eddie signed it. Then, almost out of habit, Eddie started to put the pen in his pocket.

"Shall I arrest you for stealing my pen?" Jarrod said with a hint of humour.

"Was just looking after it for you as you know, there are a lot of crooks in here!" Eddie grinned at him.

Even Jarrod had to admit it was pretty funny and laughed.

"One more thing, Eddie," Jarrod's voice took on a serious tone. "If I ever found out that you talked, you know that the consequences of breaking the Official Secrets Act are very severe. Do you understand?"

"I do," Eddie replied, appreciating the gravity of the situation.

"Right, Now, here's what will happen. Tomorrow a police car will come for you. You'll be taken to my office claiming you're to be interviewed for an ongoing investigation. After you've finished, we'll bring you back here. Oh, and Eddie, don't worry, I haven't forgotten about your family," Jarrod said as he was leaving.

To Eddie, Jarrod was a decent officer. Hard but fair. He knew that if Jarrod had said he'd try to help his family, then he would.

Jarrod got back to the office and looked for Peter. Asking him to make sure a laptop that had a wi-fi connection to his printer was in a locked interview room. After seeing everything was prepared, he took the evidence bag with the stick back to the evidence room and left for home.

8

When Jarrod awoke the next morning, the first thing he did was to check his phone to see if there had been any messages. Relieved to see that there were none in the inbox, not even from his ex. He made his way to the kitchen. This time he made sure that he had a good breakfast. He then showered and dressed. Satisfied all was in order, he left the flat to go to work. Jarrod got to his office and made sure that the laptop was ready. He checked to see if it was connected by wi-fi by printing off a test message. All he had to do was to see if Eddie showed up to help. Eventually, Eddie turned up. Jarrod asked to be left alone with Eddie as he knew he wasn't going to be a danger and rough stuff really wasn't Eddie's style.

Eddie sat down at the desk and moved the mouse, and the laptop sprang into life.

"Eddie, you do remember what I told you yesterday that if I even hear the faintest whisper that you've talked; I'll make sure the law comes down on you like a ton of bricks," Jarrod told Eddie firmly with just a hint of menace.

"I promise, Mr Fischer," Eddie replied sounding like he was in the dock again.

"Just help my wife and kid. That's all I ask."

Eddie sat there as Jarrod handed over the stick. He sat down facing Eddie with a cup of coffee as Eddie took the stick and inserted it in the USB slot. He waited, knowing it wasn't an exact science as these things take time depending on the level of complexity. He wasn't looking at what Eddie was doing as he wanted to say I want to show you I'm helping you if you help me as I'm trying to show some trust.

After about ten minutes, Eddie sat back. He looked pale and shocked as though he'd discovered the location of the Holy Grail.

"Mr Fischer," Eddie said nervously, a little shaken after sitting back in his chair, "I think you had better come and have a look at this."

Jarrod came and moved his chair next to Eddie. He was expecting something else, but when he saw the screen, it took his breath away. Even Jarrod who had seen a lot of strange things in his life felt stunned when he saw what was on the screen. Pictures, maps, lists of people and other data. "In your opinion, Eddie, is this real?" Jarrod said trying to keep calm and suppress his shock.

"There are ways in which you can tell if something like this is real, and this ticks all the boxes. No doubt it is for real, Mr Fischer," Eddie said.

Jarrod sat there his chin resting on his fists. Truth is definitely stranger than fiction, he thought. He wanted to pinch himself to make sure he wasn't dreaming, but he knew it wasn't a dream. He spent the next few minutes going through all the material that was on the stick. Now he could see why Darren had put a cryptic lock on the system.

He went to the door, composed himself, opened it and spoke to the constable outside.

"Take our friend to the canteen and make sure he gets a good meal. Tell them I'll be along later to settle up," he said.

Eddie was taken to the canteen. While Eddie was gone, Jarrod started to print off everything that was on the stick making two copies, one for safe keeping just in case, and the other for the file. He then put the stick back into its plastic bag and took it to the evidence room as though nothing had happened; he made sure the interview room was locked before going back to his office.

Jarrod sat down, caught his breath as he tried to come to terms with everything. He knew one thing. Mossad hadn't been involved, which made things a lot easier. But who was involved? Darren must have made a very serious enemy somewhere along the line. All the documentaries Jarrod had seen he'd dismissed regarded this as a joke with expert upon expert giving their own version on this also the debunkers as Mark Twain had said, 'Truth is Stranger than fiction.' This confirmed everything he'd heard blowing away his disbelief in an instant. He slowly reached for the phone. A part of him was reluctant, but he had to speak to the Chief Constable and arrange a meeting. He liked the new Chief, and the feeling was reciprocated. A no-nonsense, straight-talking guy. Though on his days off he'd take his dogs for long walks in the beautiful Sussex countryside.

The Chief had been an officer in the army with one of the old, but lesser-known regiments. He was even a 'Captain' for three years in the SAS. When an officer joins a regiment, they can only serve three years, unlike normal ranks who serve for as long as they want, and whatever rank they held before joining the SAS they join as a Captain before reverting to their original rank. The chief had been on tour seeing service in Northern Ireland before being burnt on an undercover mission there. The mission had been to grab an informant who was in danger of being killed by his colleagues in the IRA, and they had decided to get the informant out before the IRA had killed him. It turned out it was a well-staged trap and that the informant had been working to lure him into a trap and the Captain had had to react with split-second reflexes if he wasn't going to be killed or captured as the IRA would have made great capital by having captured an SAS officer. He had killed the first gunman with a single shot from the pistol in a concealed carry jacket and driven the car fast in reverse despite the flat front tyre, thanks to a shot from the other gunman who had managed to get around the corner, and he and his fellow SAS soldier had fought a running battle until they got to an army safe house.

The Chief's mind recalled that day as it would never leave him. The briefing took place in one of the many secure rooms in the barracks in Belfast. Present was the Chief and his driver Den. The people taking the briefing was a colonel in the intelligence unit and a person in civilian clothes. No doubt a 'Spook' thought the Chief as he and his driver were briefed on Operation Sparrow Snatch.

"Gentlemen," The Colonel started, "We have a mission that is of the utmost importance. For some years we've had a mole in the IRA feeding us information. His name, for now, is 'Sparrow'. We have had word from him that things are getting worse and he feels that his colleagues in the IRA are now onto him would like to silence our informant. Our mission will be to extract him from a street in Enniskillen and bring him to a safe house for a debriefing from our colleagues in 5."

He motioned towards the gentleman sitting quietly at the back of the room.

"No one is to know about this. We have arranged for the extraction to take place in two days. Nearer the time you'll be given maps and the time for contact. So I suggest, you make yourself aware of the location and to plan your routes both Alpha and Beta routes in and out. You'll also have the location of an army house."

As soon as the chief had the maps, they started to plan the route. Firstly, the pick-up point then the return to the safe house. Photos of the area were at hand. Also, local 'safe houses' which were more like observation posts manned by soldiers with a supply of civilian clothing in case they were seen. Den spent some time going over the car they had drawn from the motor pool for this assignment. The number plates being false in case they could be traced. The Chief drew a couple of Browning HI-Power pistols and some spare magazines, and lastly, a favourite of any soldier going on a mission a lunch box for each of them plus something for the informant in case he was hungry.

The Captain and his driver had driven in the town of Enniskillen during the late afternoon. They were to pick up an informant there. He had sent an urgent message that he had to be lifted as the other members of his IRA cell were on to him. If he wasn't to be killed, he had to be extracted. The car drove into one of the backstreets ready for the meeting. The sound of Billy Joel singing 'We didn't start the fire' was coming from a radio somewhere in the background. The plan was to take him to an army safe house that was ready and mind him until he could be sent to a security service location for eventual debriefing.

"There he is, boss!" said Den, the Chief's driver as he saw a lone man, slowly walked towards the car along the still wet pavement after the rain earlier that day.

Den was a corporal and had joined while in the Parachute Regiment. He had seen service in the Falklands War when the helicopter in which he was flying crashed during a blizzard during the operation to retake South Georgia. He had also been one of those involved in the Pebble Island raid which resulted in some Argentine aircraft being destroyed thus giving the troops landing at San Carlos a better chance of establishing a secure beachhead before taking Stanley. He enjoyed working with the Boss as they had made a good partnership in the three years the Chief had been with the SAS.

The Chief started to feel a bit uncomfortable as he started to sense something wrong.

"Thanks, Den, make sure the car is in reverse just in case," he said to Den.

There was something about the way the man was walking alone along the pavement towards them that made the Chief suspicious. The informant was holding something in his pocket which made the Chief nervous. He looked up at the upper windows of the houses and saw curtains move one of them; the window opened. He reached for the gun in his shoulder holster slowly changing the safety switch from safe to live. The engine was running as was the drill. His fingers ready to pull the gun - a Browning HI power pistol - out of his holster under the left side of his jacket. The man on the pavement pulled his weapon out and aimed at Den and the Chief with both hands. The Chief pulled the gun and shot him in the head through the windscreen. That split-second decision separated the living from the dead. They could have been killed, wounded or taken prisoner as 'celebrities' and eventually murdered in some quiet woodland back road.

Den stepped on the accelerator. The car sped off backwards leaving traces of rubber and the smoke from the tyres. Another gunman came out of hiding, shouldered his Kalashnikov and fired a short burst one of the rounds hitting the nearside front tyre. Thanks to Den's driving the car backwards had driven around the corner with a flat front. He managed to turn the car around and headed off at speed but crashed into a parked car just as the IRA gunmen ran around the corner. Both the Chief and Den used the car for cover as they fired at the gunmen. Shooting a gunman dead and hitting another before leaving the safety of the car. They both forced their way through a house, much to the surprise and shock of the people living there, making their way into the back garden over a wall and quickly finding their directions, headed towards the safe house. The army team that was manning the house readied themselves for possible action as they watched in surprise two men rush up the drive and found sanctuary waiting in the house. The Chief had pulled out his ID as he was making his way to the door if that hadn't been opened by the soldiers inside the Chief would have used his Rugby experience to open the door and which the soldiers inside manning the safe house to their relief were glad to see ushering them quickly inside as one of them had his pistol ready while keeping an eye out for any gunmen who happened to be following. The Chief used a secure line to report HQ what had happened and sought for an immediate extraction.

They sat at the table in the warm sanctuary of the kitchen. Both men, while they were waiting for that extraction enjoyed a warm cup of tea as they started to calm down after the recent event.

"Fancy a ciggy, Boss?" Den said as he lit a cigarette and offered one to the Chief.

"On your bike, Den! Heard these things could kill you. Would murder for a shot of single malt whiskey, though," Chief said knowing that being an active, safe house and listening post for this area it would be dry.

"Only if you're buying, boss!" Den said with a huge smile as a single malt whiskey was a favourite tipple of Den's.

Long after he retired from the Army, whenever he drank a shot of whiskey he remembered with affection his time with 'The Boss.'

"Dream on, Den! Don't be daft; they don't pay us enough for whiskey!!" the chief said in good humour. Being in the SAS normal Army protocols for example as in addressing different ranks went out of the window. Den had enjoyed working with the boss. He was sad as he knew their working relationship would be coming to an end and that they had got on very well. Next stop after their debriefing by Army Intelligence would be a discreet return to Hereford home of 22 SAS or known affectionately as 'The Hooligans' by other regiments in the British Army.

The Captain's cover had now been blown which meant he had to leave Belfast, Northern Ireland and wouldn't be able to return as his face was now well known to the IRA. The Chief had been given choices by the intelligence team based on his experiences after being debriefed. Return to the Army somewhere behind a desk, join a security firm or the Police. He chose the latter as that had been what his Father had been in. His father had been pleased as any proud parent at his passing out parade. A little disappointed he hadn't been a Police officer but still proud. Maybe somewhere his father would be smiling knowing his son had finally become a Police officer.

"Hello, Sir, it's Jarrod. I was wondering if I could pop up to see as I need some advice," Jarrod said.

"Any idea what time?" the Chief asked.

"Well, anytime would be good as long as it's okay with you," Jarrod replied.

Killer Bytes

"Can you come up as soon as possible I've got a free day?"

"I'll be up as soon as possible, Sir," Jarrod told him.

Jarrod went to the canteen and paid for what Eddie had for his meal. As he was on his way out, he saw Eddie and went up to him. The two officers discreetly moved out of the way.

"Thank you, Eddie. I've appreciated your help, and I haven't forgotten my side of the bargain. I'll see what I can arrange with social services as soon as I can," Jarrod told him.

Before long both Jarrod and Eddie were making their way to Lewes. One returning to prison and the other to the office of the Chief Constable. Jarrod took a deep breath as he knocked on his door.

"Enter," the authoritative voice said.

Jarrod entered his office with a case folder. Both men shook hands.

"Now Jarrod, what dragged you all the way from that nice seaside office of yours to see me?" the Chief asked.

"I think its best we go somewhere quiet," Jarrod said.

Of course, he knew the room wasn't bugged, but he was just taking precautions in case someone walks in. They went to one of the many meeting rooms around the building. Normally reserved for one to one meetings or formal interviews. They each took a seat round the table. Jarrod sat next to the Chief and opened the folder. He showed him what has happened over the last few days. Showed him the file on Greg and what was on the memory stick told him and how the bullet could only have come from a Glock. After a while of reading, the Chief sighed, closed the file leaned back in the chair looking out of the window at the countryside. He thought for a few moments and started to speak.

"You know that I was in the Army and involved in various exchange programmes. Occasionally, you would pick up whispers of things at official functions or during off moments, nothing much, just snippets, then people once they had realised they'd said something would hush up. Never direct, just hints and rumours. I'd watch TV shows where there would be theories on this put forward but then ridiculed. Until today I thought this was just it, the product of an overactive imagination and entertainment. It also confirms the whispers I'd heard. Jarrod, I'm going to have to call this one in with those higher up asking for some guidance on this. I'd like you to carry on with the murder investigation keeping me up to speed while I take this higher up the chain of command," he told Jarrod, "The thought of a 'ghost' killing someone is very disturbing."

Jarrod drove back to his office unaware of what was going to happen next. At the same time as Jarrod had been talking with the Chief, another type of meeting was taking place but very different. Tash had gone to the chapel of rest at to pay her respects to Darren before the funeral. She carried the flowers to place on top of his coffin, holding them tightly the thought of letting them fall on the ground wouldn't have been right. Her body is shaking with fear, nerves and loss. She knew that despite everything Darren had liked some things to be done properly. Ali along with one of her friends, Cassy had gone with her for support. They entered the chapel.

The coffin was surrounded by candles whose light reflected on the coffin. As soon as Tash saw the coffin, she fell apart. Ali and Cassy helping her as the flood of tears flowed like a river from her eyes. Even Ali, who normally gave the impression that he was a strong person who had a tear fall slowly down his cheek. Tash recovered her composure and placed the flowers on the closed coffin. At that moment on that typical cloudy Autumn day, the shone through the cloud bathing the chapel with many colours from stained glass windows bathing the coffin in colour.

"You daft, stupid bugger! Knew that there was something wrong with that stick you gave me," she said quietly and sternly to the coffin, hoping that even in death Darren would hear her telling him off.

"I'll always love you and wear your ring. There will only be you, Darren," she said as Ali and Cassy remained a discreet distance behind.

Ali, before he left stood in front of the coffin bowed his head, touched the coffin and then left with Tash and her friend.

9

It was the day of Darren's funeral. The solitary bell tolled calling the people. As John Donne had written *For Whom the Bell Tolls. It tolls for me.* A large number of people had wanted to attend including Jarrod. He felt that as he was leading the investigation, it was his job to be there. To say I'm here and I'm on the job. The funeral service in the church was very emotional. Everyone was recounting what a great person, team colleague and friend he was, telling funny stories which brought a smile to everyone. Ali, in his address, had been emotional occasionally wiping a tear from his eyes, which for Ali was rare.

After he finished, he went and bowed his head in front of Darren's coffin. It was strange that the only person who had been able to control themselves at the funeral was Tash. After her little speech, she went to his coffin and whispered to it. Darren had loved music, and one of his friends had sung 'Eben? Ne Andro Lontana' from the opera *La Wally* that had been a particular favourite of Darren's along with other pieces of opera, including the famous 'One fine day' from Puccini's *Madam Butterfly*. As Darren had said, only Maria Callas could bring a tear to his eye. That seemed to bring tears to many people's eyes. Nobody saw the tear that fell from her eyes onto the coffin and after giving the coffin one last touch of her hand along with a farewell kiss for the man she truly loved. Tash walked back to her place with her parents, who were there for her, giving her strength and the support she needed to help her through this trying day. They even had managed somehow to track down a cousin of Darren.

As they were going outside to the internment, Jarrod noticed Tash - recognising her from the photo supplied from records after she had been brought in after that Breach of the Peace - supported by her friends while she laid red roses on his coffin before it was lowered in the ground. Ali, Mike, Warren and others were nearby offering that comfort and support which those who were closest could give. Greg was also there, well at the back with his shades on so he could see the faces in the crowd better. Not that he would be grieving but if the Police were there and also who was closest to Tash. He noticed Jarrod as he had done a few days previously.

After the service, they all went to a pub to celebrate in typical Carewise style, Darren's life. Greg was there pretending to be shocked, giving the impression of a good workmate. He felt it would look dangerous and suspicious if he weren't. The wake lasted well into the late evening. Tash had been given some days off as compassionate leave. Mike had held her hand telling her the usual 'We're here for you, anytime just speak to us if there's anything we can do' line.

"Hi. I'm Rob. I knew Darren for a short while. I just can't believe it," Greg told Tash at a suitable moment giving the impression of a stunned grieving friend and colleague.

"Thanks, mate," she said in an understanding way, yet she was still an emotional dam ready to burst.

Greg in a way admired Tash the way that she was holding it as best as she could.

"You know, I've been there before," Greg said as he recalled that day in his mind when he went to see the family of his friend Ryan, who died just for some worthless mound of dirt and how he went to see his family as a friend would.

After he came home, he went to visit Ryan's family. That lonely walk up from the pavement to the door. A short walk, but it seemed to take an age. He adjusted his beret and black armband still holding some of Ryan's personal effects. How he tried to tell his family and his little brother, but the words never came. He'd just sat there and gave Ryan's effects including the dog tags still bearing the marks of battle to the young brother called Kyle.

"What was he like?" the boy asked.

"He was my friend and a good soldier," Greg told him.

"When I grow up I want to be a soldier just like Ryan."

"You know Kyle, the world's seen too much war and death. When you grow up, why don't you do something to help people instead, like being a doctor and find a cure for Cancer or AIDS or become an inventor?"

The flag with its thirteen folds was later given as the 'gift' of a grateful nation in the triangular wooden box to be put in the living room. A photo of Ryan was on a nearby table. Black tape on one corner.

"Semper Fi Bro! Adios Mon Hombre," Greg had quietly said that day in respect to a friend and brother-in-arms.

"Anytime you need someone; I'm here for you. I'll give you my cell sorry, my mobile number. I guess many of you Brits would get the wrong idea," he said trying to get some rapport with a joke.

Through the tears and smudged makeup, Tash tried her best to smile. She searched her handbag still in a daze looking for a pen and paper. She quickly wrote her number down thrusting the piece of paper into Greg's hand and then tidying up her honey blonde hair that had become all mussed. Greg smiled which gave Tash some comfort and sense of security. He'd text her tonight just to show her someone was out there. Just as Greg was about to walk away a large guy with unkempt curly hair and beard came up to Tash to see her.

"Hi, babe!" Warren said as they hugged each other firmly, "What can I say? Just that I'm here for you as I was for Darren."

"Oooo, Wazza, you're such a good mate," Tash said to him.

They hugged firmly again as old friends do before Warren left; Greg suddenly latched on that there was someone else. Not that he'd known this, but he'd still call this in just to keep The Controller up to date. Greg walked away and off home. Still no closer to finding what he was after maybe, yet a possibility there was a chance that she could be hiding something like this other guy. When he was in bed that night, he sent Tash a text to which she replied. Next, he sent The Controller a text. The message he got was something he was expecting. Take out the two of them after finding what they have. How many times has it been used? Orders are Orders? A lot. Many of those who used that phrase got the justice they deserved at the end of a rope at Nuremberg. As he slept, he drifted back to a tent somewhere in Iraq.

The large tent was full of armed soldiers patiently waiting for details of the upcoming mission. Even though the conflict was nearly over, there still were roles for the recon unit and their skills. The searing heat of the desert made its presence felt even in the tent it made the briefing difficult but nothing that was serious enough. A young officer stood in front of the large group of men sitting intently gazing at him upon hearing on what the new mission was and what was expected of them.

"Men," He started off, "The mission for later is going to be a tough one! We have had reliable intel from the CIA that there's a store of WMDs about 50 clicks west of Tikrit. We have been informed by intel that enemy forces have stored a stockpile of Sarin there and it's guarded by a complement of The Republican guard. Our job is to make this secure for Coalition Command and to hold till the disposal team arrives."

Rumblings came from the group as they still had not found the WMDs they were looking for despite the numerous leads they'd had which was the reason in the first place was why the UN had granted a mandate enabling the Coalition the authority to invade Iraq which the politicians from the coalition countries had been so passionate about in order to secure the mandate from the UN and support from their own peoples. Also, they knew that the Republican Guard would be no pushover as they were Saddam's elite soldiers and had been in the forefront of fighting during the war with Iran.

They saw a map showing the site in red. A larger layout of the base taken by airborne recon showing a possible location where the weapons were believed to be stored. Notes were taken of what was said. On a table near the front was a model of the complex with a question mark on where it was thought the stockpiled nerve agents were being stored within the base.

"We will take off at 21:30 Zulu to gain the element of surprise. The Blackhawks will drop us at an LZ about five clicks short of the target. Cochrane, you'll take your team and flank around the East side giving covering fire while Barnes you'll take the west side." The officer ordered pointing to the map. "Once we make the base secure I don't want anyone touching anything till the weapons experts are brought in. I want you to take a good lookout at the model beforehand. We'll call up the Hawks afterwards to take out any wounded and prisoners for debriefing. Up to our departure time, I want you to prep and make sure everything works. Get some chow and rest."

The men started to move out after they had taken a look at the model and started to make familiar the layout of the complex. They knew the drill. All of them had prepared for the worst-letters and wills for loved ones.

"Central Intelligence Agency! Wow! That's a contradiction in terms Bro," Ryan said to Greg as they were both cleaning their weapons at a table under camouflaged netting which gave some respite from the desert heat.

Various parts of their weapons lay on the table ready to be inspected and cleaned. Greg paused to take it all in. He'd come a long way since joining the Army trying to find a direction as a lot of young people struggle with. Sergeant Major Cochrane - the equivalent of Warrant officer in the British Army - he'd become through hard work and found an ability within himself to inspire and lead the men who were under him. He liked Ryan as he could see a lot of his younger self in Ryan who was already a Corporal.

"My dad was in Nam, and he told me that screw-ups were a common occurrence. Lots of friendly fire. There were a lot of casualties because of it," Greg told Ryan.

"I heard that too," Ryan said.

"You okay, Ryan?" Greg asked his friend.

"I know from what we've been through it seems kind of routine, but I've got a feeling, bro," Ryan confessed.

"Hey! Remember that time in the swamp when we were at Benning?" Greg said trying to take his friend's mind off the thought he might not make it back.

"Yeah, I was on point and got pricked by this object that was floating in the water, and I thought it was a snake," Ryan said.

"Turned out it was a branch!!" Greg said, "Poor branch."

Ryan remembered that time when the unit was on exercise going through a swamp. Near chest high. They were arcing their weapons from side to side while still looking through the sights. Faces painted to blend in with the foliage. Ryan was on point as they slowly made their way through the swamp. Greg not far from Ryan. Ryan was noticing something long and brown on the surface. Ryan's eyes started to open wide in terror as it came closer.

"Aaaah!" Yelled Ryan as the object 'bit' him.

Greg quickly went to him; the others were looking concerned.

"Snakebite," Ryan said, fearing the worst.

Greg pulled the object close showing Ryan it was only a branch. The rest of the team laughed including Greg and Ryan.

"Let's take the branch out on a casevac!!!" Greg said in good humour.

Both men laughed. Later after all the preparations they joined the rest of the chalk and stood by a Humvee and had a group photo the sort that soldiers had done in so many conflicts before. Greg stood next to Ryan and mockingly made the Devil's horns above Ryan's head. For some that day, it would be their last sunset. As Zulu time drew near, men were aware of this and had already made their confessions or were making peace with their God. As it was a well-known quote that there's no such thing as an atheist in a foxhole which, in many times as these when soldiers are about to go over the top that even the most fervent non-believer will sometimes turn to prayer in their own way. The Sun was slowly setting, and the men were doing their last-minute checks making sure they and each other were ready. Putting camo cream on their faces, Greg made sure his chalk was ready. He went to stores and drew out some M72 LAW projectiles giving them to some of his chalk.

"Good luck, bro," Ryan said to Greg as they fist bumped each other on the way to the Blackhawks.

"You too, man!" Greg replied.

"If anything happens I'd want you to tell my family?" Ryan asked Greg.

"Come on, man, we're going to cruise it. No shit!" Greg said to raise Ryan's hopes.

As the teams boarded the helicopters, they were asked to take a pill supposedly to counter the effects of any nerve or chemical weapons. Once inside the men threw them away as they were not too happy after hearing rumours about the reliability of the drugs the US military were using.

Both men knew that this was going to be no walk over and that the Republican Guard were mean hombres and it hadn't been long since Iraq had finished an eight-year war with their neighbour Iran. A war- that had turned out to be a modern replay of World War one which quickly moved

from a mobile war to static trench warfare and stalemate-
which the West had initially supported Saddam as anyone
who was taking on the Ayatollah Khomeini at that time was
the number one antagonist in their eyes and, as the old
saying went, 'The enemy of my enemy is my friend.' It
wasn't until the usage of Chemical weapons on Iranians
and parts of Iraq that the mood in the West started to slowly
turn against Saddam and the politicians who once had
praised Saddam and were now turning away from him just
as they had done to Sir Arthur Harris over the bombing of
Dresden in 1945 despite the politicians at the time
clamouring for one last show of force against Hitler's Third
Reich.

The soldiers started getting on board the helicopters,
slowly, the Hawks took off banking and heading north
towards their LZ the men lost in thought. Each man
concentrating on his task as well being lost in silent
prayers. The sound of the helicopter's engines and the noise
coming from the cockpit made it difficult to relax as the
formation headed northwards. When the Blackhawks
arrived, the men started to disembark the choppers and
move out. They were heading to the point where they
would split into two groups readying themselves for the
assault. In the distance they could see and hear the
explosions of battle knowing shortly they would contribute
in a smaller way to the sea of battle that had been
enveloping the Iraqi nation like a flood. Greg who had
studied English at high school remembered the parting in
the play 'Julius Caesar', between Cassius and Brutus before
the battle of Philippi a long time ago yet still poignant
today as it must have been in every battle in history. 'The
end of the day will come, and the end will be known. If we

meet again, we shall smile, but if not why then this parting was well made.' Death was waiting as well as Charon the ferryman who would be ready to take the pennies from the eyes of the dead for payment to cross the river.

The next day they began to take stock of the cost from the battle though, it could hardly be called a battle more like a skirmish. It had been bad for both of the teams. Together they both lost and bled heavily. Barnes' team had lost four including their chalk leader Sergeant Barnes while Greg's team had lost seven including Ryan. It turned out that despite a thorough search there were no WMDs again, another screw up paid for with the lives of brave people. Tired and dirty the men of both teams got ready to move out after they had secured and searched the compound and like the other leads for these weapons again just nothing — another dead end for the Coalition in a war that would be known for its faulty intelligence.

Greg, his face dirty from the camo cream the smoke of battle and moist with sweat matting his shortish black hair looking like some grotesque demon from the depths of hell as he stood by the line of black body bags waiting for their silent turn to begin the process of being repatriated. Even in death, there was a protocol to be observed. Greg took his helmet off and shouldered his weapon as he slowly knelt down to touch his friend's bag. Tears started to fall. His head bent in respect to a fallen brother in arms and friend.

"Always remember you, bro!" Greg said sadly, "I'll make a point to visit your family."

"Cochrane!" The lieutenant's voiced called out. "Get yourself on that Hawk. You're needed at Baghdad airport ASAP! Before you ask why don't, even I don't know," the Lieutenant said.

Greg bade his friend a final sorrowful farewell.

"Till we meet again, Bro! Adios!" he said as he stood up and turned to the waiting Blackhawk that was to take him to Baghdad airport where the coalition was based before the terrifying endgame of Operation Iraqi Freedom was to be played out. He strapped himself in and leaned back closing his eyes as the chopper made its way to Baghdad and, like the travelling Blackhawk, his life would also now take a new direction.

******

April 8th 2003

The sounds of a coalition and Iraqi gunfire echoing through the buildings as the battle for the city was drawing near to its final bloody endgame was no different to the Red Army when they took Berlin at the end of World War II except that this time there were no atrocities carried out. The leading armoured elements of the 3rd Infantry Division drew in towards Firdos Square near the centre of Baghdad where the statue of Saddam would later be torn down to the jubilant cries of the people. While Iraqi officials claimed that the coalition was being beaten elsewhere and that no allied tank would ever enter the city despite the 'reassuring' Information Minister Muhammed Saeed al-Sahhaf or

Baghdad Bob as he was known, on the roof of a building watching the M1 Abrams tanks entering the square. The coalition was winning. At what cost? The war was ending. But would the war really end, and who would be the victors?

10

Greg was sitting at a table in a tent at Baghdad Airport. He'd had the luxury of a shower to wash away the stain of war to cleanse himself and to feel like a new person although it was as if he was baptised anew when he arrived. His rifle nearby on the table. A mug of coffee sat on the table along with a plate of hot food. To him this seemed like Heaven after the last few days. A Major with folders and coffee in a battered metal mug that carried a near faded yellow shield that had a double ended match on it entered. Greg snapped to attention.

"At ease, son. Sit down," said the Major to reassure Greg as he drew up a chair. "Hear you had it bad out there."

"Could say that. Lost my friend Ryan. For what? A small fucking trench system with a machine gun a few clicks from our drop off point. We were told by intel that it was a storage facility for WMDs. What was found? NOTHING! We lost good men for fuck all!" Greg was pissed off and angry he wanted to lash out at anyone who had helped in killing the men he knew and had trained only to be killed for some trenches.

"Son, it happens all the time. We had similar when I was with the 196th in Nam during Operation Cedar Falls in an area along the River Tinh we called The Iron Triangle. That was a shit operation despite the historians saying it was a victory. You know who I am?"

"Sir! Major Bradley Battalion Intel, Sir!"

I'm retiring from the Army shortly and I was wondering about your plans, son," he asked as he sat down next to Greg.

The Major opened a file and moved it so both of them could look at the contents of the folder. After Operation Iraqi Freedom had been declared a 'victory' by the coalition Greg had been allowed to take part in armed patrols in the city to make sure all was secure and there were no Iraqi soldiers taking part in resistance activities against the coalition. He saw first-hand the smashed buildings showing the might and force of precision weapons and the explosive power within them. The blood all around which hadn't been cleaned away. Somehow in amongst the destruction caused by war he could hear the sound of children playing. He admired how kids can somehow be the most vulnerable yet somehow, have the ability to survive and endure. All he could do was watch.

He remembered the history lessons of how the war in Europe had finished leaving Germany smashed but yet like a Phoenix, had risen from the ashes and had grown to be a major economic power with the help of foreign workers not as slave labour but as gastarbeiters or the 'guestworkers' who'd been invited to come to the new Germany to take part in its rebirth. The film of how the allies defied the Russians and flown in supplies to keep West Berlin running and free. The stories of how aircrews would drop sweets and presents for Berlin's children during that time as the planes from the free world flew in to Tempelhof airport to unload their supplies and then head back to get another load for the free people of West Berlin. As he rode in the Humvee his mind recalled another part of his history classes by remembering the quote from Tacitus that was about another war a long time ago that happened in Germany sometime in the second century AD long before the nightmare of the second world war when the Roman army had defeated the Germanic tribes at great cost after a lengthy campaign 'Solitudinem faciunt pacem appellant – They make a desolation yet they call it Peace,' *how true,* thought Greg who did not gloat or take any pleasure from his part of what had happened. They say that history is always written by the victors. He wondered what would be written about this conflict for future generations to learn from.

The deep abyss of sleep took Greg into its depths giving him a temporary relief from the nightmare of the war.

11

The next day was a free day for Greg. He went for a walk to the seafront. Yes, there was something about a British seafront. The salt air assaulting his senses, the sound of the waves crashing on the shore and the sound of the water as it drew back through the stones. It gave him a chance to escape to a peaceful feeling. It was on this walk that Greg passed the beautiful Church of St Paul of Tarsus just up from the seafront. One of the famous Wagner churches and buildings that sprang up in the 1800s in the Brighton area built to help the poorer people go to church and avoid paying pew tax. Something made him pause and drew him inside. It had been a long time since he'd been inside a church let alone an Anglican one. It was as he was growing up dealing with the rigours of student and teenage life and preparing to think about a future career that he had started to drift away from the church.

Even though he'd left the church, God had never left him. He quietly sat down on one of the pews in the church and turned to prayer, despite the sounds of chairs scraping the floor and people whispering, which was something he hadn't done for years. The smell of hot wax filled his senses as well as the fading smells of polish and incense. He looked round to see what he was looking for. He got up slowly, went to the votive stand and lit a candle. Saying a prayer, crossing himself he then went to the confessional to confess his sins to the waiting priest inside. He noticed the stand by the confessional telling people that Fr Felix Smith was the priest taking confession that day.

"In the name of the Father, and of the Son, and of the Holy Spirit. Amen," fr. Felix said while crossing himself as Greg entered the booth.

"I confess to almighty God, to his Holy Church and to you, through my own fault that I have sinned in thought and word and deed, and in things I have left undone. Bless me, Father for I have sinned. It's been years since my last confession".

"And what is it you have done?" the priest asked gently through the mesh as he reverently kissed his stole before hearing Greg's confession.

Greg was hesitant but wanted to say the sins he had committed he opened his mouth, but nothing came out. As Greg sat down, he noticed the carving of a rose. Sub Rosa or, literally beneath the rose to reassure people that what they say is bound by a code and that anything they say will stay between them, the priest and God.

Greg began his confession about what had happened during the firefight. The anger as he saw his friends killed and the rage with those who had caused it by ordering them on the mission. Greg told the priest about what had happened in other incidents though when it came to killings the words wouldn't come out. The part about the mercy killing during the mission had been what was burning him up inside the most. Greg was hesitant to tell him this. It weighed down on his shoulders the most. Greg felt puzzled. Why did God want him to feel like this just about this particular killing and not the others? What was God trying to say to him? Telling the priest about the other things had helped.

The priest after a while gave Greg an absolution though he insisted that true forgiveness can only come from God, and he asked him to read the passage from the Bible, Mathew 18 vs 18. Greg got up and left, and in a way, felt relieved. He made a mental note that he would retire after this assignment hoping that the Controller being a fellow soldier would understand and when he did, he would ask God to help him follow a path closer to Him and hoped that he could show God that he was truly sorry and penitent that he trusted God for his forgiveness.

A week later, Greg was back at work. His eyes scanned the call centre floor looking to see if he could find Tash. His eyes found her. She was surrounded by her friends, each giving her a positive boost. His eyes connected with hers. A smile of thanks came his way. He hoped to meet her during the lunch time to start getting close. Who was that guy she was with at the wake? It had been a hard morning for Greg as he'd had nothing but complaints about appliances and the engineers. Since Greg had started he'd moved quickly onto the complaints section of his team dealing with unhappy clients that had issues with the repairs or, the lack of them. Greg had spent the morning chasing the suppliers and been given the run around by them. He felt tired. Jokingly, he thought of taking a contract out on them as well. Greg stretched back in his chair and started to log out for his lunch break. Then, he saw Tash walking to the break out area. He managed to catch her eye. Finishing quickly, he stood up and went to her.

"Hi! How's it going?" he asked.

"Oooooh, you could have given me a funny turn, don't want too many people dying here in a short time," Tash said with a faint smile.

Greg liked the attempt at gallows humour. It was something about the British sense of humour he liked. The rawness, the schoolboy way people laughed at things that really weren't all that funny. They spent the time chatting about how Tash was coping since the loss of Darren. Phishing, hoping to elicit something from Tash that would reveal what Darren gave to her Greg was starting to get fond of her even though he had a job to do. Placing himself in Darren's shoes, he would have made copies of what he'd hacked. Shame the police had to be there otherwise he'd have had time to search the room just in case there was something. *If I'd been Darren*, Greg thought, *I'd have given a copy to Tash.*

"If you want to meet up after work for a drink, then it would be a lot better than chatting here," Greg said.

"You know, I'd like that. All this quiet, thinking Darren's going to turn up when I know he's gone for good," said Tash carefully holding back the emotion.

"Let me know when it's good for you," he said empathically.

"You're really sweet. You're such a lovely guy. You know that?" Tash told him.

Greg gave the faux blushing embarrassed look, which seemed to do the trick. They both went back to their desks for the next half of the day.

Tash sent Greg a text asking if they could meet up a few days later. She was going to meet Warren but felt that she could do with a drink, and something more than coffee. Tash sent Warren a text that she was going for a drink instead and could they meet at the weekend for a coffee. Warren agreed and said that he hoped she had a good time. Warren had been fond of Tash and thought that Darren and Tash had been a well-suited couple. But something in his mind was troubling him. Like all of us, that feeling of dread we have when someone is walking over your grave. He tried to put his finger on it but couldn't. Like when he met Darren with Greg that night outside the office before they went for a late coffee and chat. It was giving him great unease.

He tried to sleep, but even though he did all he could, he was restless. Up every few hours. He'd never been like this before. There was something about Greg he didn't like. He wasn't anti-American. Warren tried to put it out of his mind as the product of an overactive imagination. To satisfy his curiosity, he'd follow Greg at a reasonable distance and see where he lived.

The next evening, he waited over the road in the shadows of a turning off the main road near Carewise to see Greg and which way he went. He saw him exit the building, waited and followed not too close and not too far. He followed him to his lodgings in one of the squares facing the sea made a note and walked home. Greg was not as naïve as Warren had thought. He often would slip into a doorway just to make sure he wasn't being followed and saw Warren following behind him. He didn't mind as he wondered how Warren would explain this. He smiled to himself as he continued to his room.

Tash was getting ready for her drink with Greg, and since Darren's funeral she could do with spending it with someone who wasn't fussing and asking her how she was. It felt so good like a stone off her shoulders. She spent a while getting ready making sure her makeup was just right, and it went well with the simple but smart look she had chosen. A darkish grey pullover with a black rose embroidered on it, with a short black skirt, opaque tights and flat casual shoes. Tash smiled as she pronounced herself ready with a breezy 'Ta Daa!'

"You really look good, girl," she said to her reflection, "Not too tarty but you're going to have a good time, girl."

She walked to the pub as it was close to her home. A good choice as she felt going to a club or large pub wasn't on her mind at the moment and wanted somewhere comfortable yet wasn't crowded that was one thing she couldn't deal with just now. She smiled as she saw Greg dressed casually but smart standing outside thinking *What a star*!

"Hey, you look good!" Greg said trying to make her feel relaxed.

"You scrub up well too." She kissed him gently on the cheek as they both went into the pub.

They ordered their drinks and went to sit in a quiet corner.

"How was your day then, Tash?" Greg asked as she sipped her glass of wine.

"Okay, it was a rota day as tomorrow so, I just did the usual housework; did some shopping and the washing. Tomorrow I'm going to visit Darren. He'd like that," Tash told Greg.

They talked about everything during the evening as Greg had plied her with wine. At the end of the evening, Tash lost her balance slightly as she stood up giggling as she did. Greg had caught her. Tash, due to the amount of drink, the warmth of the pub felt secure as Greg briefly held her. She looked up fixed her eyes on Greg and drew her lips close to him as they melted into a warm passionate kiss.

"Come on. I'll make you a coffee." She drew Greg by the hand to her home.

"Oh God," she said as the wall of cool air slapped her face. "I still can't get over it that he's gone. I've still got his memory stick which he asked me to look after."

Greg's ears pricked up when she said that. He wasn't drunk, but had only sipped a little and thrown away the rest of his drink each time.

"Memory stick?" Greg asked.

"Naughty boy, I wasn't supposed to tell you that, cos I neeeed Wazza to help me with it first," Tash said laughing in her inebriated state, slurring her words and not realising what she was saying unknowingly had signed her own death warrant.

Greg knew that he was on the right path and played along with Tash. As they got to the door, they began to embrace and kiss wildly fumbling to open the door while looking at each other. The door opened, and they rushed to the sofa continuing their frenzied kissing. Soon they were in bed making love.

Greg woke up early in the morning, and got slowly out of bed, careful not to disturb Tash as she was lying, gently sleeping on her left side with her hand stretched out to where Greg should have been, went to the bathroom and nearly slipped on the wet floor. On the way back to bed he checked his jacket to see if his bag was there in his inner pocket. As he pulled his hand out of his jacket pocket something caught his eye. To a normal person, the two books slightly sticking out would not have meant anything, but to Greg it did. He went over to the books and pulling them out found the memory stick hidden at the back. He reached in and retrieved it.

"Bingo!!" he said softly smiling and put the stick in his pocket, replaced the books and went back to bed. Not long after, Tash was slowly stirring and snuggling up to Greg whispered in his ear.

"Mmm morning!" she said as a person whose nightmare had seemed to have left them and could look forward now to brighter things. She knew Darren would understand and would only want her to be happy.

117

"Fancy a coffee?" she said in a half-tired way.

"You bet," said Greg.

"Just you wait there, lover boy, and I'll get it for you," said Tash as she gently kissed him.

Greg watched as she went to the kitchen, got up and waited behind the door.

"Owwwww!" he said in loud but not too loud a way.

"You oka……."

The word okay was never finished as she didn't see the blow to her neck which killed her instantly. She fell like a rag doll to the ground. Crumpled. Silent. Still. Greg stood over her for a moment and quietly said a prayer before taking her body to the bathroom to make it look like she had broken her neck when she slipped on the wet floor. When they found her body the amount of alcohol in her system would make people think that she'd had too much to drink and fallen over on the wet floor breaking her neck.

Greg shaved. Carefully making sure that nothing was left in the sink however, one tiny clipping fell unnoticed to the floor unseen yet powerfully loud. Happy he'd done everything he made a coffee. Took a towel and had started to wipe the areas he had touched. Carefully he dressed. Took the used condom with him. He left the bed as it was, just to make it convincing to anyone who came. Making sure there was some water on the floor in the bathroom. He looked at Tash's body for a second. The open eyes and slightly open mouth.

He left. As he shut the door, he made sure for a second there was quiet. His hand drew away from the handle and taking off his latex gloves, walked home. Now, he would get his haircut and later text The Controller. Smiling he walked home via the barber.

Warren had woken up with a jolt. Though he couldn't place or put his finger he had that moment of dread as though something was about to happen or had. He grabbed his mobile from beside his bed and sent a text to Tash. No reply, which for Tash, was the norm. Tash was always slow went it came to answering a text, so no worries. It wasn't till nine in the evening that he was getting concerned, another text. Still nothing. Perhaps she'd had too much to drink and was the worse for wear and knowing Tash that was very possible. Still, tomorrow being another day, he could always visit her.

The next day Warren decided to visit Tash as he was getting worried about her. In the past Tash had never taken this long to reply despite a heavy night. Maybe he was too caring, but when you have a lovely friend as Tash you can never take things too lightly, especially after what she'd been through lately. He reached the flats where she lived. Outwardly it was a typical building that had been built at the end of the nineteenth century, yet inside it was divided into flats. Each one being comfortable and very desirable for the young. Tash had been lucky to have parents to help her with it.

After being let in by one of Tash's neighbours, Warren climbed the stairs to her flat. It was a journey he'd often taken and never stopped feeling happy to visit his friend in her lovely apartment. Today, however, that was all going to change. Forever.

He got to the door. Knocked and waited. Again, he knocked but no response. He knew that she was at home as he asked a mutual friend via a text who worked with her to see if she was at the office and they told him that she was meant to be off. Even when she was out shopping or visiting she would send a reply.

"TASH!" he called out. No reply.

"Hello, Warren," said Mrs Smyth - but was always known as Jules to friends - who lived opposite who was surprised with the way Warren had been trying to get an answer from Tash's flat.

"Oh, hello, Jules," Warren said. "I'm a bit worried as I've heard nothing from Tash."

"I heard some activity some time ago but since then, nothing, Warren," Jules told him. "Hang on, I've got a key which Tash gave me."

Jules went into her flat using her hand that held a cigarette to move her long red brown hair behind her ear. A flat that she and Tash along with Warren had used so many times when they used to have a mug of tea together and sort the world to rights always turning a dull sad time to finish with tears of laughter and returned with the spare key to the flat that she kept for Tash just in case she had locked herself out.

"Let's open up," Warren said.

They opened the floor and were both greeted by a strange smell. They looked round found the bedroom a mess which for Tash wasn't new. A scream pierced the silence. Warren rushed to the bathroom and found the reason why Jules had screamed. They found Tash lying on the bathroom floor since the morning after her date with Greg.

Warren pulled out his phone from a pocket, dialled and waited for an answer.
"Can I have the police?" Warren spoke into his mobile trying to find the words, trembling with shock and struggling with the finding his friend dead on the floor. The words were hard to come and as well coherently. "I'd like to report a death," he nervously said.

Not long after they called the Police, they arrived. A sense of shock overcame them as they found Tash lying dead on the bathroom floor, despite the training they get; after all, Police officers are only human. Warren and Jules were both sensible to realise that they would have to leave the flat as soon as they had reported it in. They sat at the table in Jules' flat in disbelief a mug of tea and biscuits for Warren and coffee for Jules as she sat there finishing off her ciggy. This was a time for them to comfort each other as they had just lost their dear friend. It was also to preserve the crime scene more than anything as well as trying to steady their nerves to help the Police with their investigation.

The two police officers had taken Warren and Jules into different rooms to take down their statements. As they were finishing writing down Warren's statement, Warren decided that it was time to get things off his chest. He needed to tell someone his worries and suspicions however innocent they might be.

"My name's Warren McBain. I'm a friend, or was, of Darren Radcliffe and Tash," he said now in a calmer tone of voice, or as calm as anyone could be in the circumstances. The officer looked up.

"I need to speak to the person in charge of investigating Darren's death."

Not long after, Warren was heading to the Police station, not as a suspect but as someone who wanted to help the investigation. He sat in the interview room. He hadn't been charged to which he felt relieved and an officer was standing in the room with him. A cup of tea sat in front of him, which Warren sombrely drank from. Trying to hold back the tears for both his lovely friends gone within a short time of each other. Still so young, full of love and promise. He thought of how Tash's parents would react.

The bombshell of when they got the knock on the door thinking it was Tash but greeted by Police officers. He could only guess how their world would fall apart as the officers would break the news. He hoped, though he knew that it would be impossible at this moment and he would visit them when he could though whatever his words were and the flowers he'd bring couldn't bring Tash back.

While Warren was waiting in the interview room a SOCO officer had found the tiny clipping which had come from Greg while he had shaved. They put it in the evidence bag which would then have whatever DNA they could find analysed. The post mortem was also looking promising with traces of Greg's skin being found under some of Tash's nails. The DNA from the skin and hair later matched. Jarrod entered the room finding Warren sitting at the desk.

"Mr McBain? DCI Fischer. I believe you would like to help us with the investigation into the death of your friends?" Jarrod said reassuringly.

"It's such a shock," Warren replied, "I last saw Darren shortly before he died with his new friend."

"New friend?" Jarrod asked.

"Yes, some American guy at his work. I saw them come out of the office. I went for a drink with Darren but…."

"But what?"

"I felt there was something odd about him. I later saw him at the reception we had after Darren's funeral and he was chatting to Tash. Now she's dead."

»Carry on,« Jarrod said.

"Later, after the funeral, I followed him to his lodgings. As I said there was something about him that gave you the creeps like someone was walking over your grave. I was worried for Tash."

"Where did you follow him to Mr McBain?" Jarrod asked.

"To a lodging house in Brunswick Square. A large beige coloured building," Warren told Jarrod.

Jarrod logged into his laptop and searched online for a view of the square. Seconds later he turned the laptop round so Warren could see it.

"That's the building!!" Warren said intensely.

"Are you able to describe him?"

"He was tall, average build, dark hair with a slightly greying beard but the eyes. They will stick with me forever now."

"Excuse me, Mr McBain," Jarrod said as he started to leave the table. "I won't be long."

Jarrod walked quickly to his office to get the file on Greg. He found the file and took a photo from the file he returned to the interview room.

"Thanks for waiting. I'd like you to look at this." Jarrod carefully put the picture down on the table in front of Warren.

"Oh my God!" Warren said, "That's him!"

Jarrod sat there. You can change a person, but the eyes are always the same.

"Mr McBain, I want to thank you for coming. We might need to speak with you again, so if you could stay local at this point." Jarrod informed him.

Warren was leaving the station and it was then Jarrod found the phone number he wanted and started to dial the phone.

"Hello, am I speaking with the owner? Jarrod asked. "I am? That's great and you are? Okay, Mr Scott. Thank you. I am DCI Jarrod Fischer. Can you tell me if you've an American by the name of Gregory Cochrane staying with you? No, you said only Mr Robert Leroy Parker," Jarrod said. "Thank you, you've been most helpful. I'll be in touch again."

Jarrod was writing it down and sitting there like someone who was starting to finally figure out the where all the pieces of the jigsaw went.

Peter and Jarrod were sitting in the office alone.

"Well, Peter, I've just spoken to the owner of the building but there isn't a Cochrane only Mr Robert Leroy Parker." Jarrod looked troubled.

"What's the matter Boss?" Peter asked as he could see that Jarrod was trying to think of something.

"I'm sure that name sounds familiar, Pete, but for the life of me I can't place it," Jarrod said.

"Simple," Peter said.

Jarrod looked in a puzzled way at Peter.

"Robert LeRoy Parker was the real name of Butch Cassidy, partner of the Sundance Kid," Peter said.

"Duh!" Jarrod said as if to say how could I have been so dumb not to realise it.

Around the same time, Greg was trying the memory stick. All he had was the same thing that Jarrod had earlier. The same newspaper and each time the laughing skull as he failed to log on. He realised he'd better get close to that friend of Darren called Wazza, so he could get him in so he could open the files. He'd have to make it look like an accident after Warren had 'helped' him to get past the login. Once the Police had figured it out that they weren't accidents he would be long gone and back in the States and just disappeared.

Jarrod went back to his office and started to think. He reached for the phone and dialled.

"Hello Carewise? Can I speak with Mike Jones, please? Yes, tell him it's DCI Fischer we've met before," Jarrod said and waited. "Hello, Mike, it's DCI Fischer; we met when I broke the bad news to you about Darren Radcliffe. There's something I'd like you to do something for me. Meet up? That's good, do you know the Bell and Anchor Café? Say in an hour's time? Great, see you then I need your help in this investigation," Jarrod told Mike.

The next day Greg was leaving for home after a shift in the noisy human train of his colleagues when a Voice cried out "ROB!" Greg looked up then his image was then captured on CCTV.

Jarrod got the picture. It was a match. However, he still needed to confirm some details about where Greg was and if he was still using the room in Brunswick Square. He put together a plan to see if the suspect was still there. Jarrod later got in touch with the Chief.

"Hello Sir. Just a call to let you know that I'm getting somewhere, but I need your okay for a surveillance operation," Jarrod asked the Chief.

"Of course, go ahead. Let me know what you find," the chief told Jarrod.

Jarrod had arranged with a retired couple to have cameras and a team in the top floor window. Mr Reeves, the owner was a former CPO in the Navy and had always believed in helping the authorities when he could. It wasn't a large team as while they waited Mr Reeves and his wife kept the officers supplied with tea and sandwiches as they waited for their man.

"Been bit of a rogue this person you're looking for?" Mr Reeves asked.

"You could say that," said an officer while looking through his binoculars and trying to drink his tea.

The camera on its tripod with a telephoto lens aimed towards the boarding house where Greg was staying ready to take pictures of Greg. The officer who had seen the photo of Greg taken at Carewise didn't have to wait long as shortly the front door opened, and Greg stepped into the street. The camera whirred into life woken from its slumber as the officer pressed the button and a series of photos were taken. The officer smiled as he finished. Slowly started to pack his things as he now had the proof that Greg was still at the building. Not long after a file containing the photos was put on Jarrod's desk. Jarrod took the photos from the folder and a smile the first for some time appeared on his freshly shaven face. Jarrod slowly reached for the phone and dialled the Chief's number.

PC Orr had once again been involved as Jarrod, and the planning team wanted to know the layout of the room. Nik, who as a lad cleaned windows had volunteered. Better a window cleaner as nobody would question one or be suspicious as window cleaners were a common sight. The idea was that in case Greg had left the windows taped or, something in the door which would alert him that people had visited the flat. Nik, in his light blue hoody and his orange and white trainers, had climbed up the ladder and anyone who saw wouldn't have bothered to have given him a second glance as there were always window cleaners about. Through a crack in the curtains, Nik saw where everything was and later gave a report to Jarrod prior to any raid about the layout of Greg's room. Even though it was just an act he felt that he'd done a good job with the window. PC 610 Orr was feeling happier now, and he was glad to have volunteered as he wanted to do something being in a way closely involved since that night which now had seemed like a distant memory.

The day of the raid had come. The room where the briefing took place was full of the officers involved. There were the usual general low toned conversations as Jarrod dressed in his Kevlar jacket and dark blue overalls entered the room.

Silence. Jarrod stepped up to the lectern.

"Morning," he said to the officers present. "Thank you for attending this meeting. We shall know it as Operation Icarus. In reference to the son of Daedalus who flew too close to the sun and the wax holding the feathers of his wings together melted and he fell, crashing into the sea as well Darren Radcliffe who also flew too close to the sun and was burn."

"See? He should have flown economy." An officer quipped.

Some officers found it funny.

"Thank you." Jarrod continued with a serious look directed to where the remark had come from. "Hopefully the laugh will be on our faces after we pull the suspect".

The room was silent once more as Jarrod started to talk about the raid.

"The suspect, Mr Gregory Cochrane is no fool. Not the usual American backpacker doing the Europe thing as the impression he's given to everyone. He isn't acting on a spur of the moment hit but part of a larger plan. I've details of his life, though as we know it, it's been sketchy till now. From what we know, he's ex US military. Trained at Fort Benning Georgia alongside Delta Force, and he was a part of the American Recon system, and his company was attached to Delta. He was involved in Operation Iraqi Freedom. At that point the records start to lead to, pardon the expression, a dead end."

At that point some of the officers who had been in the army began to show some interest as it's not often you come across people who've been involved with elite soldiers especially Delta.

"It says," Jarrod continued, "that he was killed in a helicopter crash shortly after a firefight a few clicks from their jump off point. His prints were found on the night of Mr Radcliffe's murder at the murder scene. We also have suspicion he was involved with the murder of a Natasha Jones fiancée of the late Mr Radcliffe. We've located him at this property in Brunswick Square." As Jarrod pointed to the diagram fixed to the white board behind him.

"According to the owner Mr Derrick Scott, he's there as we speak. The owner has made sure that the only person present will be the suspect. He is going under the alias of Mr Robert LeRoy Parker who was better known as Butch Cassidy aka Rob to those at his work. We arranged for Carewise to give him the day off as part of a shift change. This is the layout of the room. The bed is opposite and facing the door. There is a table just inside the door and a cabinet next to the bed. Probably this where he keeps his pistol. Make no mistake he is most likely armed. Probably a

Glock. Maybe trained to use the last round for himself. At all costs he is to be taken alive. I want some justice for those close to the late Mr Radcliffe and Ms Jones. Stay focused and take care people."

Officers started to stand and move with their equipment to the non- descript vans that were parked in the station park. There were the usual gallows humour and banter.

The small convoy made its way to Brunswick square. Knowing they would park a short distance from the premise just in case the suspect was up. Jarrod checked his pistol as he had been authorised and trained to carry a firearm just in case hoping that he'd never have to fire his weapon but there was always a chance that this would be the time and he would be prepared to use it. The other armed officers were also spending their time preparing themselves for the raid. They made sure their clothing was adjusted properly or thinking to themselves praying that they would get back home to their families. No matter how much training you get an officer is still a person, not a robot. The vans pulled up. Doors were opened and then closed quietly. Men made their way to the address where Mr Scott had already opened the front door in anticipation. Jarrod was at the front where he was getting his warrant card out ready to show Mr Scott.

"Morning, Inspector Fischer," Mr Scott said very softly.

"Morning. Is our friend still here?" Jarrod asked.

"I heard him use the bathroom half an hour ago and then close the door to his room."

Mr Scott left the building in the hands of the Police unit and went to get himself a hot coffee from a nearby café. Slowly and discreetly the officers made their way up the stairs to where Greg had his room. Jarrod took a place near the door. Officers moved in a well-rehearsed choreographed routine ready to enforce the operation poised and nervous ready for that moment. Jarrod looked at the officer's eyes looking at each other. The officer with the big red key waiting for the signal. Slowly lifting up his hand. Three fingers were up. THREE. TWO. ONE. The door flew open as an officer used the key to smash the door. Bits of door splintered and fell on the floor.

"Armed Police! Stay where you are!"

Jarrod shouted as they entered the room and surrounded the still half-awake Greg as he lay in bed. Quickly he tried to reach for the Glock which was cocked and in a drawer of a bedside cabinet ready to be used. An officer kicked the cabinet over with his foot as another one pointed his gun at him. In the tussle Greg had elbowed Jarrod in the face. Soon he was on the bed face down as Jarrod was putting the handcuffs on his wrists which were already behind him forcing the backs of his hands to face each other. The reassuring click of the cuffs and Jarrod could now see the home straight and finally feel a sense of closure. It felt as though some of the weight that was on his shoulders could be less than it had been.

"Gregory Cochrane, you are now under arrest on suspicion for the murders of Darren Radcliffe and Natasha Jones. You do not have to say anything. But it may harm your defence if you do not mention when questioned something which you later rely on in court. Anything you do say may be given in evidence Do you understand?" Jarrod emphasised everything partly out of disgust for the man but in a tiny way to vent his frustration.

Greg nodded and smirked saying nothing as they led him in his pyjamas to the waiting police car. They opened the back door and made sure Greg was secured and seated in the back seat; everything was done by the book as some suspects would try to find some legal means to sue the police or to make the make arrest and any possible conviction less secure. Soon they would be on the way to the Custody unit to process Greg. Jarrod gave an officer the keys to the building to return to Mr Scott who was enjoying a hot coffee and toast in a local cafe. It hadn't lasted long yet seemed like an eternity. Jarrod thought of the poem *To see a World in a Grain of Sand and Heaven in a Wild Flower* or as they were better known as *the Auguries of Innocence* by William Blake who himself had been locked up on a charge of sedition in Chichester for insulting one of the King's soldiers in the early 1800s.

It wasn't far to the custody centre and they waited as the large roller doors made the painful journey upwards allowing the car with Greg and the officers to be swallowed up by the Custody unit. Another van containing the evidence would follow later. Once the large rollers were down, they started to leave the van. Going through the blue door to the main part of the custody unit where Greg would be processed.

Sergeant Jackie Harwood was sitting behind the imposing desk commonly known as the bridge, ready to process him. Seeing him, she felt a chill going down her spine as he was ushered to the desk to be processed. She just saw a cold unsympathetic person who had no feeling, pity or remorse within him being escorted towards her. They say the eyes are the windows to the soul. The cold dark blackness of his eyes reflected Greg's soul. The processing would now start.

Greg answered the questions short and to the point. Professional as he had been taught during the training for how to deal with being captured. Giving the name of a solicitor, which the controller had also provided him with. Then the DNA which would be used to match up with the skin found under Tash's nails. The photo taken in the booth with a white wall at its back. Not too different from the photo of him found on his army file. Soon he was in a cell. Stripped of everything except the white noddy suit that he was wearing he would just play for time. Time of which he knew he would have plenty of. Sitting there, closed eyes. He wasn't worried about the work he was causing. He'd carried out ninety percent of what he'd been sent to do. He was okay. Dreaming of the good times in his life. He wondered what had become of Ryan's brother who he tried to discourage becoming a soldier. He hoped he'd become a doctor or scientist doing something good for humanity helping lives instead of taking them.

Time was something Greg had not been aware of while in custody. The day turning into night and turning back into day. Soon, the sound of the keys being thrust into the lock and the door being opened made Greg aware of what was next. Greg stood up and then he was being escorted to interview room 3 where Jarrod, Peter and the appointed solicitor were waiting. Greg sat down at the table next to the Solicitor facing Jarrod and Peter. There was some tension in the air as Jarrod and Peter came face to face with the man who was responsible for the killings. The softness of the lilac blue walls did little to help. Jarrod made sure two cassettes were in the recorder and pressed the icon on the touch screen to start hopefully the last part of the investigation before any trial could take place.

"Time is now eleven fifteen November 28th the interview being held here at Brighton Custody Unit. Present here at the interview are myself DCI Jarrod Fischer and Detective Sergeant Peter Lomax. Would the accused please identify himself."

"My name is Gregory Cochrane," Greg said into the microphone.

"My name is Nicholas Battershill from Drapers acting as solicitor for the accused."

"Gregory Cochrane you are being held in suspicion with the murders of Mr Darren Radcliffe and Ms Natasha Jones. You were arrested November 24th at the Grosvenor Rooms Brunswick Square. Is this correct?" Jarrod said.

For a while Greg sat there without anything to say. The quiet only filled by the sound of the recorder turning and recording the empty void.

"No comment," Greg replied.

"We have reason to place you at the scene of the crime on November 3rd where you unlawfully killed Mr Darren Radcliffe and nearly inflicting harm on three other people."

"No Comment" Greg repeated.

"We have proof linking you to the murder of Ms Natasha Jones November 17th."

"No Comment" Greg repeated again.

Throughout the interview Greg was playing for more time. Knowing they had twenty-four hours before they could apply for another twenty-four hours. This was getting on for just over two hours.

Nick Battershill, the solicitor, spoke next.

"I would like to request an adjournment to confer with my client," Nick said.

"Time is now thirteen twenty-five hours. I'm now terminating the interview," Jarrod said.

Jarrod and Peter left the room with their notes and the tape leaving Greg and the solicitor alone in the interview room.

"He's one cool customer", Peter said.

"I know it's going to be a long one Peter. Anything else?" Jarrod told Peter.

"We'll have a meeting shortly, so we can get an update," Jarrod told him.

Jarrod held a short update from his team in the briefing room. They all contributed with everything that had been found to date, The DNA match from the hair that was found on the floor of the bathroom and pieces of skin found under Tash's nails. The match of the markings on the bullets from the gun. Everything was looking like a solid case against Greg.

"Peter and I are going to interview him again the day after tomorrow at ten," Jarrod said to the team.

The day of the next interview had come. Jarrod had slept well. He got up and got ready for the day. He washed and shaved. Choosing with care what he was going to wear. Not that he usually worried about power dressing but he wanted to say I'm in control to Greg. Yesterday was your day NOW this is mine. I'm going to be in charge. He planned in his mind the strategy almost like a game of chess. The opening gambit and checkmate to him. He sat down at the glass table with his breakfast overlooking the Brighton seafront. No mocking no cockiness. Just a desire to see Greg brought to trial and justice for the families of Darren and Tash.

He recalled the moment in his mind as he had walked up the path to the home of Tash's parents to break the news knowing that Tash had walked the same path herself so many times. The reaction when Jarrod, with the police officer saw her mother, her world falling apart at the seams who had a gut feeling that there had been bad news as soon as she saw them. As they sat in the living room Jarrod saw the photos of Tash with her parents and Darren were all around the room. The scream from her mother. A mother's cry after the loss of her daughter, her only beloved child. Her husband had held his wife giving the impression that he was taking it better than she was. Ready to let it out later in private, but that was the outside look. The realisation that they would never go to her wedding and the fun of wedding plans and shopping for the big day or the proud father walking Tash down the aisle in her wedding dress and have them visit with their children. You can never see the body and soul being churned up inside. As soon as they had left there would be more crying and shouting. He wanted to hold them but being a professional he held back.

He left the home wondering at the coldness of this person who could just kill like that without realising that there were others involved family and friends alike who would be devastated and hurt at the loss of someone so full of life and whose parents should have been planning a wedding rather than a funeral. That this person had robbed them of walking Tash down the aisle going shopping for the wedding and being grandparents all without a second thought.

He sent a text to Peter telling him he'd be at the custody unit at nine thirty. Peter replied with a simple *See you later boss*.

As Jarrod drew up in the car park, Peter was already waiting as he had only just arrived.

"Morning, boss! Looks like it's going to be a good day," Peter said.

"You bet. Let's grab a coffee then we're ready," Jarrod said in a confident way.

The desk was busy and not even a glance as they made their way to the interview room. Empty. Jarrod and Peter waited. An hour later nobody had come. Jarrod was starting to get concerned. He went to the cell. That too was empty, and he made his way to the desk.

Jarrod faced the desk sergeant.

"Excuse me, I was supposed to be have had an interview at ten with the accused Cochrane who's in cell six?" Jarrod asked.

"Hasn't anyone told you?"

"Told me what?"

"Everyone's gone to Lewes. The accused left with various people twenty minutes before you arrived. I thought you knew," the sergeant told Jarrod. Jarrod, discreetly fuming found Peter in the foyer.

"I'm off to Lewes. Pete, I want you to go to the office and see if there are any messages. I'll call as soon as I know something."

Peter left for the office while Jarrod drove to Lewes. He was thinking as he drove to the Chief's office. What's going on? Trying to concentrate on the driving for the moment.

The drive didn't take long. Jarrod turned into the carpark and noticed the cars parked in the visitor's area. Even a car with CD plate on the back. Jarrod breezed through the doors and met the receptionist.

"Hello, DCI Fischer, can you go straight to the Chief's office he's expecting you," she said.

Jarrod headed for the office thinking, *What's happening*? Everyone knows more than me. His walk quickened as he approached the office. A knock on the door followed by the Chief opening the door. The room was full. Mainly people in suits drinking either coffee or tea. He could see Greg sitting smugly in a corner with his solicitor and he could hear that some of the group were Americans and others who looked like they were happier hiding away in the shadows of the corridors of power. Greg briefly saw him and gave Jarrod a look of mocking contempt.

"Jarrod, so nice of you to come. Could I meet you in the meeting room where we talked before? Be with you shortly," the chief asked with a diplomatic smile as he closed the door on Jarrod.

Jarrod made a slow lonely walk to the room as though he was back at school waiting to have a word with his house tutor. He quietly entered the room and sat at the table. Not even a coffee just a file of papers in front of him quietly waiting for the Chief. Turning over in his mind everything. Trying to make sense of today. Definitely something is very wrong. Something is rotten in the state of Lewes Jarrod mused to himself. He remembered the quote from Stephen Decatur the American naval officer who said in that famous after dinner speech: "Our Country, in her dealings with foreign nations, may she always be in the right; but our country, right or wrong". Jarrod heard the footsteps sound out in the lonely corridor as the Chief walked down the corridor from his office to the meeting room.

"Jarrod, sorry about the wait. I've asked my PA to bring us some coffee," the chief said.

Seconds later, the PA brought them both coffees. They settled down. A short silence began this informal meeting

"Jarrod can I say I don't blame you at all. Two young people murdered even though it now appears that the late Darren Radcliffe had been into computers, hacking and the Americans want it to be hushed up. It seems that 'our friends' across the pond have asked the powers that be here to hand over Cochrane. I'm fuming as well. Though they did send their condolences to the next of kin," the Chief said as Jarrod looked at the Chief in astonishment.

"How very gracious of them to let us do their dirty work by passing on condolences which just tripped off their tongue and no doubt dismissed without a thought 'I have my orders, too. I'd love to take this man through the courts and let him rot in some cell forgotten and alone. But, 'the powers that be' have been leaned on and, in turn, so have I. He's to be taken to Heathrow and put on a flight back to the States where his own people will deal with him. Some of the 'Gentlemen' here are from various parts of our government and they will accompany 'our guests' to the airport. I'm sorry that you had to find out this way, but my hands are tied. I tried leaving a message with the desk sergeant at custody, but fate intervened, and you didn't get it in time. I can only apologise Jarrod." The Chief finished as he gave Jarrod the 'I'm sorry I did what I could' look.

"That's very nice of them. To send their condolences to be passed on. No flowers. Nothing. Her parents grieving and emotionally battered without a visit from them to do it personally just for us to do their dirty work for them. How very gracious of them!" Jarrod was trying to be angry without shouting down the walls.

"Jarrod. I agree. Don't be angry with me," the chief said.

"Sorry Sir, I didn't mean to take it out on you. Not your fault I feel we've put in the work and come away without a result for those closest to the two victims," Jarrod told the Chief.

Jarrod tried to accept everything but knew that there was no appeal. Greg would be going shortly to the airport. Families, grieving without any sense of justice just empty condolences from the people who sent him on his mission. He could imagine the anger and rage from the friends and family when they found out. What words can make up for their loss?

"Isn't there anyway we could try and detain him?" Jarrod said.

"How? There's nothing we can do. I've been over this with the legal team who've told me that whatever we do we won't succeed. I'm sure if we tried to make statements there would be a "D" notice slapped on us very quickly. Quicker than we could breathe to prevent us from issuing a statement to the press and the public. It was tough getting the local media to hold out as long as they did. Jarrod, I'd like you to go back to the office and try and wrap things up as best you can," the chief told Jarrod. The Chief got up from his chair and walked back to his office full to deal with the people there leaving Jarrod to tidy things up.

12

It had been a good flight. Greg once more looked forward to stepping back on his native soil. Once through customs he'd been met by two members of 'The Firm' and, after a drive through the lush beautiful state of Virginia had arrived at the destination a non-descript building outside DC which the firm used to mostly debrief people who've been on an assignment. He entered the building with his minders who stepped to one side as Greg walked along the long foyer as The Controller stood waiting at the other end. No emotion, he was waiting like a head teacher for a meeting with an errant student. Silently, like a statue his arms folded as he watched Greg walk towards him. Once more dressed in a dark suit white shirt and a blue Paisley tie. Greg's footsteps echoing in the quiet near deserted foyer.

"Welcome Home, Greg. I trust you had a pleasant flight," the controller said in a very business-like manner as close to any fondness as possible.

Greg approached him without any emotion, receiving only a firm handshake.

"Glad to be home, sir," Greg replied a little more relaxed now he was on home soil.

"I guess we can start talking after you've freshened up," the controller told him as he and Greg went through the doors.

Along a grey featureless corridor. Sterile in all ways no feeling of being wanted. But then, whenever he came back there was never any mention of 'nice to see you'. He followed the Controller as he stopped at a door turned the handle and motioned Greg inside. It was like a motel room. A double bed. TV though there was little choice of programmes. Another door that led to a bathroom where he could wash and feel cleansed and righteous in his eyes very similar to the first time he met the Controller all those years ago at the airport outside Baghdad. He saw clean clothes neatly laid on the bed. He opened the windows as far as they could go a few centimetres only.

"Ok Greg. If you get yourself ready. There's the coffee and the milk's in the fridge. I'll be along the corridor in A15 when you're ready," the controller told him.

Once the controller left Greg started to shed himself of the clothes he'd been wearing and took himself into the shower. Stepping in the flowing hot water he started to feel good as he cleaned himself. After a while he stepped out of the shower, dried himself and dressed. Then, when Greg felt he was ready he made himself a coffee. The taste of proper coffee caressing his taste buds and mixed with the biscotti that was on the plate near the coffee machine. He sat in the armchair looking at the Virginia countryside as he drank his coffee. After he finished Greg stood up and took the card for the door opened the door and after he shut the door walked to A15. He knocked.

"Enter," the voice behind the door said.

Greg entered, and the Controller motioned him to the waiting chair in front of his desk. The Controller had opened the file ready. Papers relating to the operation were in front of him.

"So, Greg," the controller said.

Greg slowly walked to the desk ready for his own time of trial.

"Let's start at the beginning," the controller said in his *I'm in charge* tone.

Greg realised the debrief was not going to be just a quiet chat but something more intense. Every single detail from the very start to the very end and up to returning to the Firm's offices here outside the D.C. As Greg had known the Controller from his army days as Battalion Intelligence officer, Greg knew that he was a thorough individual despite the quiet persona and the meeting at Baghdad airport where the Controller had arranged a new life for him by making him vanish as a victim of an alleged helicopter crash. If anyone had asked and wanted to take the risk in a hostile land and see the remains of a burnt-out chopper they were welcome though the location of the 'wreckage' had been lost. The end of the first day had come. Time had passed and the only way for Greg to know that was the way the day was drawing to the end with the red light of the day's dying sun painting the area outside the window a reddish colour.

Greg retreated back to his room where the room had been cleaned ready for his return. He threw the dark grey jacket on the armchair. He sat on the side of the bed to take his shoes and socks off. Taking off his shirt and trousers and carefully hanging them up. He then slipped in between the sheets closing his eyes ready to sleep not caring if the nightmare of war would return. Tomorrow would be another round of questions and his story of his time in Brighton.

A few days had passed where he was debriefed by the Controller. Finally, the debrief was over. The relief, knowing he could at last go home and relax by the sea. After another day of relaxing at the facility he continued his journey to his beach side home. Once at the airport he was reunited with his car and began a two-hour drive to his home. Music playing in the background. The music from a classic rock station played John Fogerty's 'Fortunate Son' out loud but Greg stretched out his arm and turned the volume up, so he could enjoy the music with the sound of the engine going faster. This was worth the wait. The surge of the engine mixed with classic rock.

> 'Some folks inherit star spangled eyes,
> Ooh, they send you down to war, Lord,
> And when you ask them, "How much should we give?"
> Ooh, they only answer More! More! More! Yoh,......'

Boy! How he felt that was so appropriate. He was beginning to feel fortunate after everything. He remembered his dad playing it all the time and when asked his dad would say it was one of those songs that was played in Nam around the time he fought in Hue during the Tet Offensive. His dad never talked much about Nam except with the pictures and artefacts from his time there. How he smiled as he had gotten away with the crime. No more British police with their out of date way of doing things.

Maybe, one day he'd get a new passport and visit Brighton again. In its own unique way, it had charm something which America didn't. The way he'd stood at the promenade looking out at sea with the wind blowing in his face and the waves crashing on the shore. The lovely south lanes all had their appeal.

He had picked up another of his favourite cars a GT Shelby 350 which he had driven to the airport not that long ago, but to him it seemed like an age. It was the way it handled, the growl of the engine every inch a man's car feeling reassured by being at home and in his favourite car. The music coming out of the speakers. Greg put his foot down on the accelerator and the car pulled out and faster towards home. Eventually, he was near home and drove along the quiet road that led off from the highway to his home.

Nearly home and back to his favourite chair. He noticed the two walkers walking towards him along the quiet road which cut its way through the forest. Smiling and waving at them as he drove along the road ready to see the home he hadn't seen for some time. He parked the car in the garage and went inside.

The explosion tore into the tranquil fabric. The noise and explosion ripping through the tranquillity ending nature's innocence along with Greg and his home. The walkers stood and quietly looked at each other then turned towards the area where the noise of the explosion had come from and which had been once a home. Seeing a column of smoke rising into the sky they paused, turned to look at each other before they disappeared into the forest.

Greg lay on the ground dying. He slipped into darkness returning once and, for the final time to the firefight in the desert.

"Ryan, Get the fucker with that machine gun. Two O'clock, bro!' Greg yelled.

"He's gone, man," said a member of the chalk through the noise and heat of battle.

Greg turned and looked through his night vision goggles and saw Ryan's lifeless form on the desert floor. No time for grieving now, later maybe if they made it out of there. *Ryan, I'll visit your family when I get home, bro!* Greg thought as he edged closer to the source of the gunfire. Red tracer rounds flew above his head. He pulled an M72 LAW launcher from his backpack. He pulled the pin at the back, then pulled out the back half, releasing the safety and flipping up the sight he was ready. He took aim and pressed the trigger and WOOOOOOOOSH! The projectile was on its way. The explosion and noise filled the night creating for that instant an island of day in the ocean of night as debris fell around Greg, instinctively covering his head till it was still.

Soon, stillness, all was quiet he could see flames dancing in the night instead of tracer rounds, he risked it and slowly stood up. He turned 'round and noticed members of the chalk taking his lead and starting to get up from the ground. Greg noticed this and immediately clenched his fist in that moment when he felt he was trapped in a bubble as though he was there but not there. He could feel his pulse through his gloves and the sound of his breathing in a stillness which seemed surreal in the midst of battle. The squad froze like statues. Greg gave the signal to lie prone and wait, the other soldiers lying back on the ground waiting for his lead to follow. Taking his M4, he grabbed a new magazine from a pouch and throwing the empty one away he tapped the fresh magazine against his helmet so that the rounds were seated properly or else the gun could jam.

Pushing the magazine till it gently clicked into place. Soldiers never slam a magazine into place that's purely for the movies; Unlike the movies, they rarely say "Lock and Load". He then switched on the laser sight which cut a beam in the night that he could see in his night vision goggles as he slowly went forward to the trench line. He flipped the selector switch from SAFE to short burst. Carefully, he stepped down into the trench as though descending into the jaws of a devouring abyss that he might never come out from and that would jealously keep him. Pausing, holding his weapon up to his face he looked left and right before cautiously going towards where the machine gun was. His face washed by the green light of the night vision trying to catch sight of a trip wire. He trod carefully and slowly in a choreographed way.

Concentrating. Each step might have been his last, but he knew it was a risk every grunt took. Before he turned the corner to where the source of the fire was he turned 'round with his raised weapon making sure he was alone and there was no one behind him he turned to where he was going and, as he did so, Greg undid the cover on his side arm which was on his upper leg. The black grip of his berretta ready to be grasped just in case.

Greg turned the corner turning into the light from the fire his weapon had caused. Painted by the glow from the flames he stood there frozen and then saw what power his weapon had had. The young man mangled and broken. Bloodied in his last gasping breaths trying to reach for something. Greg slowly shouldered his M4, took off his helmet, and he saw, and reached for, what the young man wanted. A photo of three people. The happy young man with a woman wearing her Hajib and both of them smiling together with their young child. It was a photo recognised by fathers everywhere. He gently brought the photo to him and, as he did, slowly reaching down for his pistol. He drew the pistol making sure the young soldier only saw the photo as he brought the muzzle to the back of the young man's head.

The survivors of the Chalk heard the single shot and rushing forward, they found Greg sitting on the ground looking at the dead soldier whose arms he had just folded across his chest he'd read the ID which was in Arabic and English. Amer, 23 years old. By profession a baker. Greg had put the photo and the ID in the pocket of the young man's army jacket. There would be crying later when a woman would have a visit from a senior army officer to tell of her loss. He'd slowly closed his eyes with his fingers. Both would be at peace though for one it would come much later.

Greg briefly returned to the real world before another darkness overcame him. He thought of a young boy dressed as a cowboy playing with his friends many years ago in small town America. He asked himself what happened to that young boy? Where did he go? If only he thought what would have happened if I hadn't joined up?

He recited a prayer for the dying as the darkness swamped over him like the sea, slipping deeper ever deeper into that eternal inky black abyss towards a rest and peace he knew would surely come and be ready for judgement.

"My Lord and Saviour, in your arms I am safe; keep me…….."

The Controller was sitting at his desk when the buzzer from his secretary sprang the phone into life. He picked it up.

"Yes, Mary?" the controller said, "I see, was anyone else killed? No? Good. Then make arrangements. I think Arlington would be appropriate. Yes, and send flowers to his mother. I'll call her now and send our condolences."

As he heard a silent ping on the phone, he picked up the mobile to read the message. A knowing smile broke the seriousness of his normally quiet sober authoritarian features. He put the mobile down and started to call Greg's mother.

Later a report would appear in a local newspaper.
Sarasota FL (AP) Last night a fire swept through the offices of Mackinleys. A local law firm. Reports say that an electrical fault caused the fire which completely gutted the office. No one was hurt.

Two weeks later there had been another funeral and unlike the funerals of Darren and Tash; this one was a more sedate and formal affair in that grey cloudy day in the cemetery at Arlington where the fallen leaves create nature's carpet of autumnal colours. The group sitting to the side of the grave.

The priest standing at the head of the coffin in front of a large photo of Greg. The honour guard standing behind the funeral group ready to pay their respects to a fellow brother in arms. The Controller stepped up from his chair next to Greg's mother who he was helping her in her hour of need and stood beside the priest.

"I want to thank you for coming today to give thanks for the life of our dear brother Greg who is now being laid to rest after being taken from us in that tragic accident. Greg was an extraordinary man. A man who served his country to the fullest measure of devotion and like his father had also done in Vietnam now so many years ago. A war which people today try with zeal and misguided passion try to make America look the bad guy and belittle the sacrifice of so many of our brave servicemen and women in that conflict.

I myself served three tours in Vietnam where we all came from little towns and all of us were proud, whatever the rank, to be called a 'Grunt' as a 'Grunt' can hack it. Anyone who has any doubts of the love from our nation to the fallen in Vietnam had better visit the wall here in Washington; there they will see the gratitude from our great nation with the flowers and the people who come to pay their respects even though they might not have had a loved one serve during the war. Just as much as the former Veterans still pay their respects to their fallen friends.

Greg came to the army as a typical young man needing direction and moulding just as the potter shapes the clay on his wheel but left a man who had helped others to make it home by his encouragement and example and gaining promotion by merit and hard work. He inspired the men under him who looked up to him when the going got tough and won the respect of all those he knew. I met Greg during that conflict in Iraq where he and others undertook hazardous missions which due to the nature of them I can only say that they were vital to the success of the Coalition forces and afterwards saw in him the qualities needed to continue serving our nation. He continued serving his country every inch the brave warrior. And now we pay our respects to Greg having faced danger and death only to have died in such a terrible tragic accident at home," The Controller paused to let the words sink in. "Sergeant Major Cochrane," he addressed the coffin in a respectful military style and posture "Semper Fi!" He walked to the coffin, bowed his head and reaching in his jacket pocket pulled out a badge. Using the side of his fist, he banged it firmly to secure it to the lid of the coffin. He took a medal from his pocket looked at it for a moment then placed it next to the badge. Bowed his head in respect towards Greg's coffin and went back to his place with the rest of the party for the rest of the service. The group listened as the priest continued the service in the Arlington cemetery and at the moment of committal a rifle volley fired into the air as the words 'Ashes to ashes, dust to dust from dust we came and to dust we shall return' were spoken.

The Controller sat in the front row looking grey as the weather that day and non-expressional as his eyes followed Greg's coffin into the ground looking at the military badge and medal fixed to the lid of the coffin. The Controller had lost count of the number of military funerals he'd been to both in the field and at home. The folded flag lay on his lap ready to give to his grieving mother. He stood by the side of the grave where Greg had been laid to rest and opened a jar of soil from Iraq and tipped it into the grave and then slowly walked off along with the rest of the group. He thought as he walked back to the car escorting and consoling Greg's mum. As he did so he wondered, 'Did the rest of the party believe my story?'

A few days later Jarrod was sitting at his desk still trying to come to terms with the recent events when the phone rang. It was his PA.

"Just thought you'd like to know the Chief Constable's on his way up," Karen said.

"Thanks, Karen," Jarrod said as he tried to tidy his desk but, gave up knowing the Chief would have to find him as he was.

The knock on the door wasn't long in coming and the Chief entered his room.

"Sit down, Jarrod," he said in the relaxing way he liked to use, seeing Jarrod slowly starting to get up. He pulled up a chair to Jarrod's desk and sat down.

"I've had a call from those in the higher up corridors of power, shall we say. Our American friend Cochrane was killed in an 'accidental' explosion at his home. They're still trying to work out how," he emphasised the word 'accidental'.

Though Jarrod didn't need to work it out, he knew powerful and shadowy figures wanted him silenced just in case he had seen what was so damning to have two people killed in the first place.

"We've been asked that no further investigation continues and the case as far as everyone's concerned, is now closed. If you could file your report and pass me a copy as soon as you can."

Jarrod realised that there was no need for an investigation into his death, as like the Chief he strongly felt that it had been no accident. He thought of what he was going to tell the next of kin.

"Oh sorry, but we can't do anymore as those higher up want the whole thing swept under the carpet."

The Chief gave him the 'I know how you feel, and I feel the same' look as he sat there.

"I know that it's been difficult, and your team have done a great job, but I know you're going to say what about the families. Don't they deserve a sense of closure? I would. It may seem like passing the buck, but I'm sure you can think of something to say, Jarrod," the Chief said as he stood up and left for his Lewes office.

After a few days Jarrod was able to write to those closest to Darren and Tash to let them know about what had happened. Jarrod tried to say as much as he could to the next of kin to give them some comfort.

In another type of service but not public. Warren had gone to a quiet spot by the lighthouse at Shoreham just down the road. It was early evening just as the Sun was starting to set creating nature's tapestry of colour that happened as the sun was setting on the canvas of sky. Darren and Warren had sometimes come to that spot with cans of lager during those warm summer days to catch the sun and escape Brighton for a while. Warren had brought with him a couple of tins of lager together with a small bottle of lighter fuel, matches and the memory stick, a hammer and a tin tray. He opened the can and drank a generous amount before lifting the tin and toasting the sky.

"Darren and Tash! To two of the best friends a man could ever have! Till we meet again my friends," Warren said emotionally.

He then placed the tray on the sand, laying the memory stick on top he smacked it two or three times with the hammer, then scraping the broken remains together into a plastic bag, he made a mini altar poured the lighter fluid over it and set light to it. As he was doing so he was thinking again of giving Darren that tip. If only he hadn't given it to him none of this would have happened at that point he broke down in tears thinking of the mess that all this had caused. His two best friends would still be alive and none of the sorrow would have cast its shadow on those he knew. Warren watched the fragments burn as though they were having their own Viking funeral, and the stick was going to its own cyber Valhalla. Warren watched as it burnt away, leaving only the acrid smell of plastic which lingered for a while. As the smoke drifted away he opened the second tin and drank that. Then scraping together the last of the blackened fragments, Warren went down to the edge of the lighthouse building and scraping a small hole buried what remained of the stick. Finally, he took the tin tray and spun it out into the sea. For an instant the sun's rays reflected the tin tray and it glowed. Then it was gone, sinking into the sea. Then, Warren walked away to catch the bus home.

Warren turned the key to open the door and smiled as he saw Ben sitting waiting for him. Warren had been on to the RSPCA about Ben shortly after Darren had been murdered and told them that as he knew the cat he felt it would be only fair to look after him rather than a stranger.

A few days later as the year was slowly, but surely drawing to its eventual end, Jarrod went to the cemetery with some flowers. He found where Darren and Tash had been laid to rest next to each other in the quiet country churchyard. Bending down he placed flowers on their graves and standing back he said a quiet prayer, trusting that they were at rest and at peace. 'Together in life and death' was written in black Roman font on the joint white headstone. Jarrod, though not really a religious man, reached forward and made the sign of the cross on the headstone before bowing his head in memory and respect.

He slowly walked away on that cold cloudy grey afternoon so typical for this time of year. On the way back to his car he passed the barren branches of the trees where shortly new life would bud. The words to W H Auden's poem

'*Funeral Blues*' came to mind. Something he'd read many years ago in an English class but one of those poems that had stuck in his mind. A poem that had been written for Auden's gay friend but now used by many people for funerals. After the recent events he stopped and gave a thoughtful look up towards the sky, asking himself the same questions as many people throughout the centuries have been doing.

He opened the old wooden gate to the old church graveyard creaking on its old frame wondering what is really going on. Best not to know, Jarrod finally said to himself as he opened the door to his car sat down and pulled out his phone. He looked for the YouTube app and started to search for the hymn that he wanted. It was '*Praise my Soul the King of Heaven*' the words of Henry Lyte set to the music of John Goss. Jarrod felt that the words in the hymn were suitable for what had happened over the past few weeks. As he closed his eyes his mind drifted back to his school assemblies where it would often be played the headmaster playing with passion on the piano while the school sang the hymn. It would now have a new meaning from now on whenever he heard it. He listened quietly to the hymn in the car before turning off his phone to start his journey home. Now he thought I might take an interest in astronomy and what lies in the heavens.

The End

Author's Note

While this is a fictional story, it must be said that there is no way to condone what Warren or Darren had been doing. Hacking first started in the mid-80s, after computers were starting to learn how to communicate with each other via a telephone dial up. Prince Philip had his account hacked at the time.

Some people may look on hacking as something that is fun, and the romantic fun behind it, as though hackers are seen as TV pirates. I'm sorry but there is no way that you can call a form of trespass fun and romantic. It is a form of violation and the same experience as when a property is burgled, the distress caused by intrusion into private files seeking access to someone's assets. Hackers are cold and uncaring, not worried about the loss caused by theft. Thankfully, today, the Police do come down hard on such people, and while some people haven't been caught, their luck will not last forever.

If you do intend to hack, thinking it's a game and for fun, beware because there are eyes watching and your luck will run out.

F.J. Hardy

Lightning Source UK Ltd.
Milton Keynes UK
UKHW010452040719

345555UK00001B/168/P

9 781732 573017